Matter of Time

Legacy Series, Book 3

PAULA KAY

ISBN: 0692434917
ISBN-13: 978-0692434918

DEDICATION

To my siblings—Jolene, Michelle, Rob and Janell.
I'm so thankful that you are also my best friends.

TABLE OF CONTENTS

CHAPTER 1

Blu took the glass of champagne offered her by one of the waitresses at the party. Looking around at all of the New York designers and people that she had admired for so long, she could hardly believe that she was finally here. It seemed a dream still. Her collection had shown without a hitch, and she could already feel the buzz about it and things to come. She spoke to a few people on her way to the ladies' room, where she hoped to just get a breath from all of the excitement.

She found herself alone and as she looked in the mirror, fixing her short spiky hair with her fingers, she thought about Jemma. Her daughter had delighted in helping her with her pink streaks this past week, mentioning that she was thinking about doing something in purple herself. Blu smiled as she remembered. Jemma was growing up so fast, and she wasn't sure that she was ready for her to be taking on her own style just yet at nine years old.

She fixed the collar on her short black jacket, smiling as she remembered the day that she'd given it to Arianna.

It had been one of her favorite pieces, made especially for her best friend, and it had fit her perfectly. After Arianna had passed away, it was the one item that she'd chosen to keep from her closet, because it reminded her so much of the good times that they'd spent together. She'd altered it to fit her much shorter physique, and had worn it tonight for luck. She knew how proud of her Arianna would have been, and that thought made her insanely happy.

She took one last look in the mirror, applied a dark red lipstick, and took a deep breath before going back out to the big party celebrating a handful of designers whose ranks she was so privileged to join. Showing her collection here at Fashion Week had been something that she never could have imagined, something she never would have been able to do had it not been for Arianna and everything that she'd done for her—left her.

She hadn't made it far outside of the restroom when she found a microphone being pushed towards her.

"Blu Foster, can I ask speak to you for a few minutes?" the eager young reporter asked.

"Sure. I guess so." Blu didn't really have a chance to think about it.

"Your label, 'black-n-blu', is getting a lot of attention tonight after that spectacular runway show. How are you feeling right now?"

The microphone was back in front of her, and it was then that she noticed the camera too. Thankful that she'd taken the time to fix her face and hair, she didn't have a moment to think about what she was going to say.

"Is it?" She tried to look normal even though her heart was pounding out of her chest. She knew it had gone well, but nothing had really sunk in yet.

"Are you serious?" the reporter was saying. "You're all over social media as the most exciting new designer to hit the runway."

Blu didn't quite know how to respond, and in the back of her mind the nagging fear was there. Am I really prepared for this? She knew that she was not, no matter how much she had thought about it. Things were going to be changing, and fast.

"So how are you feeling tonight?" the reporter was asking her again.

"Oh, sorry. I'm feeling, I don't know… A bit overwhelmed, I suppose." She tried to get it together, remembering that she was on camera. "I'm very happy that the show went well and it's amazing to be among so many talented designers. I feel very fortunate for that." God, do I sound normal or ridiculous?

"So what's next for you and 'black-n-blu'? Are you working on another collection?"

"Yes, there's always something to work on." Blu laughed when she thought about all of the sketches hanging on the walls of her workroom back at her little haven on the beach. Well, there was nothing little about the very luxurious home that Arianna had left her.

"You live in La Jolla, is that right?"

Blu froze. This was really happening. Her life, Jemma—everything she had worked so hard for so many years to keep private was about to be out there for the whole world to see. She really wasn't ready for this. She hadn't clearly thought it through, although in the back of her mind she knew what the ramifications could be. And she wanted her collection out there. It was all that she'd ever wanted—to be a designer. After years of working multiple jobs bartending, waitressing, and whatever else she could find to make ends meet for her and Jemma, she had kept the dream alive, working long hours into the night on her garments.

She turned towards the camera, wondering how she could deflect the question about where she lived, knowing that it was all there for anyone to see now anyways.

"Yes, I do live in San Diego." More general than La Jolla, she thought.

"And you were raised in New York, is that right?"

She was shocked that this reporter seemed to know so much about her. Young and eager with her research, apparently.

"Yes—but New York was a long time ago." God, please move on.

"And your family? Are they in the area and how do they feel about your success and showing at Fashion Week?"

God. This is terrible. I really need to get out of here.

Just at that moment, Blu's phone started buzzing in her handbag. She quickly retrieved it, turning to the reporter.

"I'm sorry but I have to take this call. Thank you very

much." She smiled big for the camera as the reporter thanked her for her time.

She clicked the phone on as she made her way across the room to step outside, where she could talk more freely.

"Lia," she said, excited to finally be talking to her friend in Italy. They'd been playing phone tag since before she'd left for New York, and she was dying to fill her in.

"Blu, I'm so glad I finally reached you. How are you? How was the show? Tell me everything."

Blu laughed, thinking how wonderful it was to hear her friend's voice. She'd only really spent a lot of time with Lia after Arianna's death, but then the two had become fast friends. They'd shared a common grief, Blu for her best friend and Lia for the daughter she'd only just begun to get to know. Arianna had brought them together in an unexpected way, and the two delighted in sharing their successes with one another.

"Oh, there's so much to tell. I don't even know where to start. You are still coming, yes? To San Diego? Jemma is beside herself with the excitement of having both you and Gigi at the beach at the same time."

"Yes, I can't wait to see you all. I'm not sure if Antonio will be able to make it because of some issues that have come up with the vineyard, but I'm looking so forward to spending time with you all. And seeing your collection."

It had been several months since Blu and Jemma had

last been to Tuscany to visit Lia, and the reunion would be really good for all of them.

"But tell me about the show, Blu. How did it go?" Lia asked again.

"Oh, the show was great. So crazy, really. I still can't believe that all of this has really happened to me. That it's real. Do you know that I was just interviewed for some big entertainment show?" Blu laughed while cringing inside, remembering the last questions that the reporter had been asking her.

"That's so great. I knew that you'd be spectacular. Every young girl is going to want to be wearing 'black-n-blu'. It's so incredibly exciting. So how is everything with you and Chase? And Jemma? How's my favorite little girl doing?"

"Well, Jemma's fine. You won't believe how big she's gotten. And she's turned into a bit of terror, I might add. Well even more so than the last time you saw her." Blu laughed, but in actuality Jemma's behavior lately had been really bothering her. She had to get organized with her new busy travel schedule and how to handle that with Jemma. Thank God for Victoria, who had gladly taken Jemma for the few days that Blu would be in New York busy with the show. Jemma had no complaints about Blu's being gone as long as she was able to spend the night with her best friend Claire. Blu made a mental note to pick up a nice gift for her friend for doing the huge favor.

"And Chase?"

Blu could hear the question in her friend's voice. They'd learn to tread lightly with one another. Blu had watched Lia go through a lot during the beginning of her relationship with Antonio, and she'd tried not to interfere too much. On the other hand, they both wanted the best for one another. Blu knew this and she also respected the fact that Lia knew about the walls she'd put up when it came to men. It was something that she'd been working on, but she still had a long ways to go.

"Things with Chase are fine."

"Do I hear a but?"

"No but, just—you know—taking it slow."

"Okay. Well, you have been seeing him for awhile," Lia said.

"We have, yes. But it's only recently, really, that we've started talking about anything resembling a relationship. In terms of being exclusive and all." Blu really didn't feel up to having this conversation at the moment, and was trying to think of how to get out of it without showing her annoyance. "How's everything there? How's the restaurant?"

"Good job changing the subject." Lia laughed and Blu knew that the conversation about herself and Chase would be let go for now. "Thyme is doing very well. Busy as ever since the write-up in the travel magazine a few months ago. I can hardly handle all of the business. But it's a welcome problem. We've hired more people, and it's a lot of fun being in the restaurant every day. I really do hope that you and Jemma can come to visit again soon.

We miss having you here."

"Oh, I would love that. Well, with the shows I have scheduled in Europe, that is a very strong possibility. We'll have to look at our schedules and see what we can coordinate."

"It's so great to talk to you. And Blu…I'm so excited for you, for all of the opportunities. I can't help but think how happy Ari would be for you."

Blu detected the wistfulness in Lia's voice.

"I know. I've been thinking a lot about her these past days. It's hard not to, because none of this would have happened if she hadn't believed in me. If she hadn't gotten things started for me. I owe her a lot," Blu said.

"I think you just need to worry about being happy. Whatever that means for you. Well, we both know that it's what Ari wanted for us."

"Yep, you're right." Blu peeked over her shoulder at the party going full swing inside the glass doors. "And on that note, I guess I better get back inside this party."

Lia laughed. "Oh, so I interrupted you at a big party? Why didn't you tell me? Somehow I was imagining you sitting in your PJs in the hotel room, drinking a bottle of wine."

Blu laughed. "Those were the days, huh? I guess I'm going to have to learn how to schmooze a little better now. Thanks again for calling, Lia. I can't wait to see you."

"Me too. Enjoy the rest of your night."

Blu put her phone away, checked her hair quickly in

her small mirror, and took a deep breath before heading back inside. She'd stay for one more glass of champagne, and then…The idea of PJs in her hotel room suddenly sounded perfect to her.

CHAPTER 2

Blu listened to her message from Chase again as she made her way by taxi to the airport. He was sorry that he'd missed her the other night, and was really looking forward to making her a nice dinner upon her return. She didn't believe him. She couldn't stop the thoughts from entering her mind—that he was seeing other women, sleeping around—that he was just too good to be true.

She knew that she was in dangerous territory. Something that she hadn't allowed for much of her adult life. Men were not to be trusted. If there was one thing that she'd learned, that was a fact. She'd seen a lot of bad situations when she was younger, and every single one of them had involved a handsome man. Her stomach lurched, as her thoughts turned back to the interview and what any type of media exposure could mean for her.

But as much as she'd tried to push Chase away, he kept coming for her with his endearing smile and handsome good looks. And the food. God, the food. Whoever said that food was the way to a man's heart didn't understand how amazing it was to be dating a male chef. She adored Chase's cooking and loved to watch him prepare meals for her and Jemma in the kitchen. It was the first thing that she'd loved about him, after that smile, when she and Jemma first met him as Arianna's chef at the beach house. She smiled as she thought about how funny Arianna would find it that all of her matchmaking had worked, years after her death. First Gigi and Douglas, then by some incredible miracle Lia and Antonio, and finally herself ending up with the man Arianna had called Chef Cutie-Pie the first time that they'd both met him. Time would tell, but in any case, she'd have Jemma tonight, which reminded her to give Victoria a quick call.

Jemma and Claire had become best friends during their first year of school together, and Blu was delighted to find Victoria, Claire's mom, not at all like many of the other pretentious wealthy parents from Jemma's new private school.

Blu hadn't had many good girlfriends in her life, Arianna being the one real exception, and the fact that she was almost immediately able to be herself with Victoria meant a lot to her. It was good to know someone in the area; the move from San Francisco to San Diego had been an adjustment for both her and Jemma, even though everything about the beach home that Arianna had left her was absolutely life-changing.

She waited for Victoria to pick up the phone on the other end.

"Hello."

"Hey, it's Blu. Just checking in on my way to the

airport. How's everything? How's Jemma, and is she behaving herself?" Blu laughed, knowing that the young girl really could be a handful at times. Thank God that Claire seemed to be a good influence on her, always on her best behavior, exhibiting the manners that she'd been taught from a young age.

"Jemma's great. The girls are just up in Claire's room doing makeovers on one another." Victoria laughed. "They've already raided my closet and make-up drawers several times, so I have no idea how this is going to turn out. I'll call for Jemma in a minute, but first I'm dying to hear how the show went. Tell me everything."

Blu smiled at the genuine interest in her friend's voice. Considering how closed off she was to relationships, she sure did have an amazing small circle of extremely supportive people in her life. Chase included. Even if she was unwilling to allow herself to admit it, she knew that it was true. She'd been lucky the last few years in that regard.

"Everything was so great. The show could not have gone better. I'll fill you in more when I see you, which is partly why I'm calling. My flight gets in around seven o'clock, so I thought I'd come straight there to pick up Jemma."

"The girls were actually asking me if Jemma could spend one more night. There's some kind of movie marathon on TV that they want to watch together, I think. It's fine by me if it's okay with you," Victoria said.

"Hm, well, Chase did mention something about wanting to cook me dinner tonight—"

"Say no more." Victoria cut her off. "Done. You need a night with that handsome man of yours. And I say that you need to close the deal on that one." Victoria laughed.

"Not happening tonight for sure," Blu said and laughed, knowing that her friend was referring to the fact that the two of them hadn't slept together yet. Blu had her reasons for wanting to wait. She definitely wasn't going to go there, allowing herself to feel so vulnerable, until she felt a lot more confident in their relationship. But she did think that they needed to spend time together, to talk about the other night. She was sure that she'd been right about her concerns and needed to see his face when he answered her questions.

"What am I going to do with you? You apparently don't know a good guy when he is right in front of your nose. I'm serious, Blu. He's one of the good ones," Victoria said, and for some reason Blu felt that she was speaking a certain amount of truth.

"Well, we'll see. I'm not counting him out yet, and in any case, thanks for keeping Jemma another night. I'm sure she'll be thrilled," Blu said, suddenly missing the child something fierce.

"Speaking of…someone wants to talk to you—"

"Hi, mom," Jemma said into the phone.

"Hey, kiddo. Are you being good or did you just rip the phone out of Mrs. Banks' hand?"

Blu heard Jemma's muffled apology on the other end of the phone. "Okay, I just told her I was sorry. When are you coming home?"

"I'm on my way to the airport right now."

"Is it okay if I spend the night with Claire? Please? Mom, we are dying to see this movie marathon that's on, and I promise that I'll spend the whole day with you tomorrow. Please, Mom?"

It was only just recently, and only with Claire, that Blu had relaxed just a bit when it came to who Jemma was allowed to hang around. She'd spent so many years being careful that learning to trust her at Victoria's house had been a big deal at first. Lately, she had really relaxed though, and the time apart seemed to be doing both herself and Jemma some good.

"Yes, you can. I've already talked about it with Claire's mom. But you have to promise me that you'll be on your best behavior, okay?"

"As always," Jemma said, and Blu imagined the child batting her thick long eyelashes up at her.

Blu laughed. "And I'm going to hold you to your promise for tomorrow. I'll walk over to pick you up at ten o'clock and we'll plan to spend the day together at the beach, deal?"

"Deal—"

"I missed you, kiddo," Blu said into the silence, now, at the other end of the line.

"Sorry, they're off and running." Victoria laughed.

"It's okay. I'm actually pulling up to the airport right now. Thanks for keeping Jemma while I was here—and for everything. You've been really amazing. I'll have to see if Chase can cook for the four of us one of these nights."

Victoria laughed. "Or we could actually go out for a meal and give the poor guy a chance to relax and be served for once."

Blu laughed too. "Oh, he loves cooking for us. Trust me. He wouldn't do it if that weren't the case."

"Whatever you say. Have a good flight, and we'll see you in the morning. And have a good night with Chase." Victoria added with a last laugh before hanging up.

CHAPTER 3

Settled into her comfortable seat in first class, Blu took out her phone for one final time before take-off. She'd been stalling on returning Chase's phone message, and finally just decided to send him a quick text.

About to take off. Will call you when I land. Dinner sounds great if you are still up for it.

Short and to the point. She wondered briefly if he was angry at her for not calling him back. It took a lot to make him mad. In the ten months they'd been together, she'd only really seen him angry one time, and in retrospect he'd had every right to be upset.

They had been going out for a couple months and had a nice dinner planned. Victoria's husband had taken the kids to see a movie, and Blu and Victoria had gone out for a late lunch, which turned into numerous late-afternoon drinks—which turned into Blu's getting home very late after ignoring all of Chase's texts and phone calls, well past the time he'd scheduled the dinner at his place. Finally, concerned that she'd been in an accident, he had shown up at Blu's door, waking her from a passed-out stupor, something that really wasn't very common in

Blu's usually quite sensible world.

Blu had lost her mind with anger that he was so upset. Every single wall had come up, and she couldn't handle his concern or his blaming her for her lack of respect and of just plain common courtesy.

After that night, Blu learned that Chase was not someone to be toyed with as she had done in the past with some of the men she'd dated. He didn't like being treated poorly, and if that was what she thought of him, he was having none of it. Yes, he liked her a great deal; yes, he could see a potential future there and was interested in getting to know her better, and no, he was not interested in playing games. Period. End of story.

It had taken a few days for Blu to realize that he meant everything that he'd said that night, and she spent a great deal of time convincing him to give her another chance, another occurrence that was not common for her.

Yes, they'd come a long way. As she thought about his anger that night and his words about respect, she wondered if maybe she was judging him too harshly now. Maybe you shouldn't be so quick to screw this up. She was trying to trust him, to make a real effort in this relationship.

She let her thoughts turn towards everything that had happened during her time away in New York and the success of her runway show. She still couldn't quite believe how well it had gone. Reading the paper that morning, she was stunned at the reviews that she'd received. No one had anything negative to say about her work, and all of the critics were calling her the next big designer to hit the States.

Arianna had made so much possible for her. Not just with the house and money that she'd left her in the will, but all of the contacts and things that she'd put into motion before she died. Douglas and Gigi had told her later that Arianna had spent hours talking to people and showing them the pieces that Blu had made for her over the years. Her best friend had believed in her ever since she was sewing from her small corner stool in the cramped living room of her San Francisco apartment. Blu smiled, remembering all the good times they'd shared together in that tiny little apartment.

She owed a lot of her success to Arianna. But even as she had the thought, she knew it wasn't quite right. Arianna would have hated taking credit for anything, and especially where Blu was concerned. Finally Blu had been forced to accept some help from her friend, and when it came into her life she had struggled against it for quite some time, finally realizing that there was more than just herself to think of. She had Jemma to think of too, and her daughter deserved much more than Blu had been able to give her, not just in terms of monetary things, but in terms of the amount of time that Blu hadn't been able to spend with her. Working two jobs at once before coming home to sew for half the night did not leave her energetic and happy around a small child. So she'd finally taken the leap, moving into the huge beach house in La Jolla to begin a new life for her and Jemma.

She'd not regretted a single day since then; she'd not really second-guessed the move until now. Until that interview last night, she thought. God, it really was just a matter of time. She took a deep breath, wondering who she could trust and what her next move was going to be. She knew that she'd been taking a chance making her work public, but what choice did she have, really? It was either that, or just let the dream die. In the end, she'd gone forward thinking of Jemma. And now, ironically enough, it might be the very thing that had the power to destroy them.

She willed herself to close her eyes and take a much-needed nap. She knew that she had a long evening ahead of her, assuming Chase was still up for dinner. She owed it to both of them to be as clear-headed as she could be. And she was anxious to see him. She surprised herself with this thought as she drifted off to sleep.

Blu phoned Chase as she waited for her luggage. She wanted to make it a quick call so that she could also return the message that Gigi had left her. He answered on the second ring, sounding a bit out of breath.

"Hi, babe."

Blu smiled when she heard his voice and the term of endearment that he'd just started using with her lately.

"Hey yourself. Are you running down the beach, or

why are you so out of breath?" she teased.

He laughed. "I'm just cooking you the most delicious seafood dinner that you've ever had."

"Oh, is that right?" God, she really couldn't wait to see him, to be in his arms for the kisses that he lavished on her so generously.

"That is absolutely right. I've missed you, monkey."

Another pet name—that he'd given her one night after an especially energetic game of charades with Jemma.

"I'm on my way right now. Well, about to get in a cab. Shall I come straight to your place?"

"Yes, please. Do we need to pick up Jemma?"

Blu loved the sweet relationship that had developed between her daughter and Chase. For all that Jemma was unused to having a guy around, she'd grown close to him very quickly; and although Blu had had her reservations, she could see that he'd seemed to have had a positive effect on her daughter's life.

"Nope. She's staying at Claire's for one more night," Blu said, wondering what reaction the simple statement would get from Chase.

"Oh, is she now?" She imagined his teasing smile as he asked the question.

"She is. And not to disappoint you, but I'm trying not to be dead tired—so I'm not sure how long I'll last tonight."

She didn't know when she'd be relaxed enough to

spend the night with him. He'd certainly asked her to on plenty of occasions, or at least whenever Jemma happened to be spending the night at her girlfriend's, which was often these days. She didn't think tonight would be the night, though. As much as she enjoyed their flirty banter on the phone, she still had her doubts about the unreturned phone call from the night before. She tried to push the thought out of her mind.

"Okay, listen. I'm gonna run so I can get a cab. I'll see you soon, okay?"

"Sounds good. I'll have a glass of champagne waiting for you."

"I may just be champagned out." Blu laughed.

"Never. Besides, it's my turn to celebrate your success with you."

"If you say so. See you soon." Blu clicked off the phone and handed her bag to the cab driver. She'd have just enough time for a quick phone call to Gigi.

Gigi answered the phone, sounding out of breath too. Blu laughed and didn't even give her a moment to say hello.

"What's with everyone answering the phone while running around today? What is Douglas doing to you over there?" Blu teased, knowing full well that Gigi was probably trying to clean the house or perform some specific household task that Douglas had specifically hired someone else to do.

"Who is this rude woman?" Gigi teased in turn on the other end of the line. "And exactly who else is having a hard time trying to breathe? I'd be very curious to know."

Blu laughed, delighted to finally be catching up with her friend. They too had been playing a lot of phone tag over the past few days amid all of the craziness that had become Blu's life.

Blu laughed. "Oh, I just got off the phone with Chase. He's rushing around preparing me some nice feast to eat tonight. You know, the usual."

Gigi had expressed on numerous occasions how lucky Blu was to be dating a chef. And she just really like Chase a lot, as did anyone that Blu introduced him to.

"You, my dear, do not know how lucky you are," Gigi said.

"I've eaten Douglas's cooking and it's pretty fantastic too, ya know."

"Yes, it is. But he never has time to cook. The man is way too busy with work these days. Our time coming to see you will be the most we've spent together in a few weeks." Gigi laughed but Blu thought she detected something else in her voice.

Gigi and Douglas had been married two years, and Blu knew from previous conversations with her friend that it had been a big adjustment for her to go from taking care of the Sinclair household, and then just Arianna, to having a husband who only wanted to take care of her and make her life better. Gigi still fought the idea—and Douglas on occasion—of getting a job working with another family.

"Well, I am so looking forward to seeing you both, as is Jemma. She's been talking nonstop about taking you and Lia to the beach."

"When is Lia arriving? We've been playing phone tag as well. I think she's so busy with the restaurant right now," Gigi said.

"Yes, she is very busy, and we did finally connect the other night. She's coming in the same day as you." Blu smiled, thinking about her friends. "It will be so nice to have you all here. I do love these reunions."

They had made a pact to Arianna and themselves that they would all do their best to keep in touch, and so far, they'd all done a good job of it even though they were pretty spread out in terms of location. There'd been a few trips to Italy to visit Lia and multiple visits with Gigi and Douglas at the Sausilito house; this would be the second time that Blu had hosted them all at her place at the beach. Even though she was crazy busy right now with all that was happening with her new clothing label, she was more than happy to take the time to catch up with their friends. And she felt it was important to Jemma too. In a big way, it helped them all to stay connected and remember Arianna—which had gotten less painful over the years, although she was never far from their thoughts, especially when they were all in the same place at the same time.

"What was that? Sorry." Blu realized that she had totally spaced on what Gigi was asking her.

Gigi laughed. "Are you too exhausted? We can talk later when I see you in person. I was asking you about New York. How the show went?"

"Oh, it was so great, Gigi. I can't wait to tell you everything that is happening. It's beyond my wildest dreams, really. I'll tell you all about it in person."

"I can't wait to hear. I'll let you go. Give Chase my best, and you have a good night together."

"I'm sure we will." Blu hoped so anyways. "And please give Douglas a hug for me. I can't wait to see you both soon."

CHAPTER 4

Normally Blu loved eating dinner at Chase's house. He too lived on the beach, but where he lived in Pacific Beach had a much more laid-back feel to it than her big home in La Jolla. Chase had done well for himself as a personal chef, but it wasn't the kind of lifestyle that Blu was now living. Still, their two worlds seemed to mesh well. Whenever Blu was hanging out with him at his bachelor pad on the beach, she felt, in a way, more herself. It was relaxed and the neighborhood had zero pretentiousness to it, something that Blu would have hated.

Often they'd go for a walk on the beach after eating outside on the expansive deck that Chase had added on to his home. Or they'd meander down to the boardwalk to play a few games or scream on the iconic wooden roller coaster that still saw its share of tourists during the busy season.

Tonight, though, Blu didn't feel like doing any of that. Chase had served her the most amazing seafood dish that he'd been perfecting for a local private event he'd been hired to cook for. The food was delicious, as usual, but the conversation was stilted. He'd greeted her at the door with a big deep kiss and a beautiful assortment of flowers, just the ones she loved to fill her home with. For a moment, she felt that everything would be fine, that she'd just let her doubts and annoyances go, but they kept gnawing at her throughout dinner.

Finally Chase put his fork down abruptly and turned to her. "So, what's up, Blu? Are you mad at me for something? I don't get what's going on here."

"Yes. I am, actually. I told you that I was." She was referring to the text she'd sent him after the unreturned phone calls.

'Seriously? I thought you were joking about all of that." He looked like he was trying to tease her now and for a moment, she thought it better to drop everything, to pretend like yes, she had been joking. But that wasn't her style. And how's that been working for you? she thought.

"I'm just not sure—" She looked him in the eye. "—I'm not sure that I believe you, Chase.

"You don't believe that my phone was broken?" Chase had a look on his face that she'd seen only on occasion. "Seriously, Blu, why would I lie about that?"

"Because maybe you're seeing someone else?" There, she'd said it. All of her insecurities out there, raw and open, for him to mess with.

"Blu, I'm not seeing anyone. I barely have time to work and see you. But you know that."

She could feel his approaching the end of it. All it

would take was a little push on her end of the conversation and she'd probably never see him again. Push him away forever. Was that what she wanted? Just when everything was going so well. But just when everything is about to fall apart too. The thought came quickly as she remembered the interview with the reporter the night before. God, she might as well let things be over. He'd not want anything to do with her soon enough.

Chase was up from his chair, and for a moment she thought he was about to pull her towards the door. Instead he reached for her hand, guiding her up from her chair and pulling her close to his strong chest. Her slight 5'5" frame fit perfectly, nestled against him, and she'd always felt safe when he held her tight.

He placed his finger under her chin, tilting her face to look into her eyes. "You're the only woman I'm seeing and you're the only woman I want to see. When are you going to believe that, silly? I love you, baby."

He'd only said the words once before, right before she was leaving for New York last week, and Blu had been so taken by surprise that she didn't know what to say—how to react. Tonight it caught her by surprise again, and she knew she wasn't ready. She didn't know if she'd ever be ready to trust a man that much. She looked at him now, willing herself to say something that didn't make her sound like the complete jerk that she was.

"I—I don't know what to say. I know I drive you

crazy. That I don't have a reason not to trust you," Blu said.

Chase pulled her to him, and she felt his hands make their way down her jeans to cup her butt in that flirtatious way that she loved. "Oh, you drive me crazy alright," he whispered in her ear, before she felt his lips on hers for a deep kiss that showed the passion he was ready to unleash on her.

She kissed him back before she pulled away a bit. "Let's not get too hot and heavy here, mister. I am planning to go home tonight."

He looked like a little boy who'd been reprimanded one time too many. "Woman, you just drive me plain crazy." He laughed, but she knew that there was a bit of truth to his statement.

He'd been so patient with her in terms of the level of their intimacy. It wasn't that she didn't want to sleep with him or that she hadn't had her share of lovers over the years. There had been many, for sure. But Chase was different. She felt it; and even though she kept making mistakes with him, she felt in her heart that he just might be the one for her. She didn't want to give him her whole trust—all of her—until she was sure. She knew that if she was wrong, it would ruin her forever, and she was determined not to let herself get hurt like that.

"I'm sorry. And I don't deserve you." She kissed him playfully. "How you put up with me, I'll never know."

"That's an understatement." Chase winked. "So you

believe me about the phone, and we are moving on, then?"

"Yes, and moving on to a lovely dessert, I hope." She smiled as she walked towards the kitchen to see what else Chase had prepared for them. He hadn't had as much training when it came to desserts, but she found everything he made masterful, and his chocolate surprises never failed to delight her.

He followed her into the kitchen to pour a dessert wine and collect the light mousse that had been setting in the refrigerator. "Shall we make a fire inside?"

The weather had turned just cold enough in the evening recently to enjoy the fireplace that Blu loved. They'd already shared many a conversation and their share of arguments too by that fireplace, and tonight she swore she'd end things on a good note. Maybe she'd even get the courage up to tell Chase that she loved him too. God, where did that come from? Do I love Chase? She followed him into the living room as he stopped to turn on her favorite rock music, which currently was a local band that they'd come across at a party just recently.

"So…" Chase set their glasses of wine down on the coffee table as they settled into the comfortable sofa. "Tell me about New York. I want to hear everything about the show."

"Do you?" Blu teased. It wasn't that Chase didn't have a sense of fashion. He did, and she loved how he dressed, even though she knew that he was always most comfortable in jeans and flip-flops. But it was rare for any guy that she'd ever dated to be truly interested in her clothing line or her love for design. Slowly she'd begun to share with Chase some of her passion for the clothing that she created, and he did seem truly interested to learn about it.

"You know I'm interested. And honey, I'm so proud of you."

Blu felt her face growing slightly warm at the sweet words. And he was incredibly supportive of her career. Who was she kidding? Chase was incredibly supportive of her. The most incredible man she'd ever been with by a long shot. She silently reprimanded herself for her attempted sabotage earlier. Let good things be good, Blu. It was something that Arianna had said to her once. During their last days together.

She smiled as she remembered the conversation even though with it came a pang of sudden grief for the friend that she'd lost. It was still incredible to her that it could come out of nowhere, even years later. But she'd gotten used to it. They all had—Jemma, Gigi and Douglas, Lia—and even Chase, who'd been caught totally off guard about the passing of the young woman who had employed him as her chef.

She turned to give him a deep kiss, looking in his eyes as she pulled away. "Thank you. I mean that."

He pulled her down beside him on the sofa, where they cuddled for the remainder of the evening, he listening to her recount the events of her time in New York and she, feeling wanted, feeling loved in a way that she hadn't felt before.

CHAPTER 5

"So tell me everything." Victoria said as she settled across from Blu at the little breakfast table tucked in the nook of her kitchen.

The view of the ocean from this spot was just as magnificent as from her own home, and unsurprisingly so, as her good friend lived right up the street. Blu had come to love the ease that the two women now had with one another. She still cringed when she thought about how wrong her first impression had been of the beautiful woman sitting across from her.

She'd gone to pick Jemma up from the private school that both she and Victoria's daughter Claire attended, during the child's first week of classes. She'd been running late, which was rare for her, and was mortified to see all of the other mothers, looking so put-together in their "ladies who lunch" clothes or tennis outfits from their morning matches, milling about Jemma, anxiously looking around to see who would eventually turn up for the poor girl.

Jemma, being Jemma, didn't actually seem bothered by her mom's tardiness at all, but it was Victoria who'd sent the other mothers on their way, once she saw Blu pulling up in her convertible. They'd met briefly a few days earlier; Blu had caught her eye, waving when she saw her in front of the school.

Victoria was as put together as any of them, and Blu guessed that she played tennis and lunched with the best of them, but she was immediately drawn to the woman with the dark straight hair and wide grin. It didn't go unnoticed by her, that in a lot of ways Victoria reminded her of Arianna. They definitely shared many of the same traits, and once she'd gotten to know her, she realized how unaware of her own beauty Victoria was.

Blu loved the down-to-earth quality that she possessed, and over the course of a few shared coffees learned that Victoria had not come from a wealthy background. She'd met her husband, John, while she was bartending and he was attending medical school. Blu and Victoria both laughed when they discovered that they shared fond memories and a certain hatred for their bartending days.

So the two became fast friends, and their relationship was as honest and forthcoming as any that Blu had known. Victoria had a way of helping her to put things in perspective and Blu had even come to count on her for this. She was counting on it today, in fact, because she knew that she needed some fresh perspective about her evening with Chase. Victoria did really like Chase, but she'd always seemed to be able to remain objective as well.

Victoria repeated herself as Blu gazed out the window. "I want to know about New York...about your show...about last night. Tell me everything."

"Sorry. Yes. Lots to fill you in on. Thanks again for keeping Jemma. I hope she was well-behaved."

Victoria was nodding her head. "Jemma was fine. You know them. Busy with their projects, and they did stay up pretty late watching TV last night. I hope she won't be too tired today."

"And you'd tell me if she's ever any trouble?"

"Yes, you know I would."

And Blu did believe her. She'd told her in the past about a couple incidents where Jemma had lost her temper over something, giving Claire a hard enough time that the young girl was in tears. But as with most young friendships, they were quick to make up, and Blu was very pleased that Jemma had found a best friend so quickly upon their move.

Blu settled back against her chair with the nice coffee her friend had prepared for her. The two women had a bit of time, as they'd promised Jemma and Claire that they could finish the art project they were working on before Jemma would have to leave to go home. Blu was dying to talk to Victoria anyways, so it would give the two women a chance to talk.

She filled Victoria in on everything about Fashion Week, which was a fun conversation because Victoria loved fashion as much as Blu did and knew just as much about the latest designers, if not more. Blu was constantly asking her opinion about her fabric and design ideas, and Victoria's thin 5'11" frame made her the perfect model for Blu, which was amazing for both women. She'd already designed several pieces for her, and Victoria was more than delighted to wear them around town at the many events that she was obligated to attend with her husband.

Victoria was genuinely pleased to hear all of the good news about Blu's showing. Blu could see it in her friend's face, and appreciated the excitement that matched her own enthusiasm about everything that had transpired over the past week. She had her work cut out for her, for sure, and had only just begun to think about the upcoming European shows and her travel schedule—which was going to be quite aggressive, to say the least.

"Of course you'll let me know if you need help with Jemma. Seriously, Blu, it's no problem and I'd be happy to help you out," Victoria said.

Blu smiled, thinking how helpful and gracious her friend was, but she knew that it wasn't a good long-term solution to her child-care issues with Jemma. She'd be traveling too much for that.

"You're so sweet to offer. Really. I do appreciate it. But I've got to figure something out. I probably need to hire someone that I can take with me when I'm traveling. To look after Jemma and to teach her as well."

"Oh really? Are you thinking of pulling her out of school here?"

"Well, it's not really my preference, and I doubt Jemma would love that idea either, but having a tutor might really end up being the only logical solution. I don't want to be away from her for weeks at a time, and by the looks of the shows coming up, that's what it would be." Blu sighed, thinking of everything that she had to sort out pretty quickly. Maybe Gigi and Lia would have some helpful advice for her over the next week. In any case, she'd have to go speak to one of the agencies; maybe they'd help her with some interviewing while they were in town, as it wasn't something that she was familiar with. She feared that her overly protective sensitivity would make it difficult for her to hire anyone that would be a good fit for the job.

"And what does Chase think about all of your upcoming travel?"

"Well, I haven't really told him the extent of it," Blu said thoughtfully, and felt the lurch in her stomach. It really would be hard to be gone from him so much. She sighed as if she was just at this moment realizing her feelings for him.

"What's that about?"

"What?" Blu responded, noticing the funny look on her friend's face.

"What are you not telling me about Chase?" Victoria teased. "Did something happen last night?" She quirked her eyebrow, which made Blu laugh. "As in, did you finally spend the night with him?"

"No, no. That hasn't happened yet. Much to his dismay, I'm sure," Blu said while gazing out towards the water as if collecting her next thoughts. "The man does have the patience of a saint. I will say that about him." She laughed lightly.

"Well, I think that he respects your wishes. It does say a lot that he hasn't been pushy with you. I mean, it's not as if you've not slept with guys before, so he must wonder a little bit what's up. Not that it's any of my business, of course."

"Hey, it's not as if I have a reputation for sleeping around, you know," Blu said, lightly slapping her friend on the leg in a teasing way.

"Oh, I know. That's not what I'm saying. Really."

"I know. I'm just kidding. It's hard to explain, I guess. I just feel like waiting with Chase is better." She felt her face growing warm and felt a bit embarrassed with her friend, which was unusual for Blu, typically pretty vocal and outspoken about pretty much any subject including sex. At least when Jemma wasn't within earshot.

"Hey, I get it. You like him. A lot, Blu. It's okay to admit it, you know." Victoria was smiling at her.

"I guess I do. Yes. I just don't want to mess it up. I really think he's one of the best things that's ever happened to me. And I—I guess I do worry that either I'm going to get too close to him and then end up out of my mind when he leaves me. Or I'm going to push him away before that can happen." Blu didn't know why she had sudden tears threatening.

"Hey, you're not going to do that. And it doesn't have to end up being either of those things, you know. It is possible that everything in your life is going right, including this amazing relationship that you are in. But I think you're going to have to let go of some of that worry to really give it a chance."

"I know. Chase says as much to me himself. Somehow I seem to push to a certain point and it's only because of him that he doesn't let it go so far—so far that he won't come back, I mean."

"He's a keeper, Blu. And I think he really adores you." Victoria was grinning widely, as if daring Blu to disagree with her.

"He told me that he loved me again last night." Blu said this quietly, as if afraid that Jemma might be lurking nearby waiting to hear her mother's deepest secrets.

"Blu. Trust your heart. Go on. Love him back. I think that whatever you are fearing is the worst thing that could happen is much less of a concern than your not taking a chance with him at all."

"You're probably right." Blu said. But she doesn't know all my secrets. The things that no one knows, the things that I'm sure Chase can't accept.

"I know I'm right," Victoria said with a laugh.

"Well you did manage to land yourself a heart surgeon

that's pretty hunky. So I suppose you know something about falling in love." Blu laughed, knowing from Victoria that she and John were still pretty frisky in the bedroom, even after twelve years of marriage.

"Hey, we've had our share of problems to work out. No marriage, or relationship, is perfect. Just remember that and you'll be fine."

"Thanks for the advice. I'll be sure to take everything into consideration." Blu laughed, happy that she'd had the time to talk about some of her concerns with her friend. "Now I better round up Jemma if we have any chance of making it to the beach today. She's certainly not acting like she missed me very much, is she?"

"Oh, you know kids. They are such self-involved little creatures—Claire included in that statement most of the time."

The two woman laughed as Victoria crossed the room to the intercom to buzz the girls upstairs, convincing Jemma to come down with her things after much protesting.

CHAPTER 6

Blu and Jemma walked up the slight incline from the Banks' home to their own a bit further up the hill, Blu listening to Jemma's excited chatter as she filled her mom in on all the news and everything that she and Claire had been doing together the past few days.

"Mom, see that bus stop over there?"

Blu was slightly distracted, half listening to her daughter and half thinking about her to-do list for the next week.

"That's where we got the bus with Nathalie," Jemma said.

"Wait—what?" Blu's attention was fully back on Jemma again. "Victoria let you take the bus?" Nathalie was Claire's fifteen-year-old sister and Blu knew her to be very responsible, but still the thought of the girls taking the bus made her stomach lurch. She'd loosened up quite a bit when it came to how protective she was with Jemma, but she would have thought that taking the bus would have been something that Victoria would have cleared with her first.

"Where did you girls go on the bus?"

"To the mall. Nathalie had to return something, and Claire and I thought it sounded like a good adventure."

"I'll bet it was." Blu said carefully. "And Victoria couldn't take you?"

"No, she was going to but we just decided to go on the bus. Mom, Nathalie does it all the time with her friends."

"I know, sweetie, but Nathalie is much older than you and Claire."

"She's not much older. Mom, I'm not a baby, ya know." Jemma was pouting now, and Blu wanted to try to lighten the mood so that they could enjoy the rest of the day together.

"Honey, I'm not saying that you're a baby. It's normal for a mom to be worried about her kid, you know." She reached over and gently tugged the end of Jemma's ponytail.

"Well, I don't think you need to worry so much." She reached out to take Blu's hand, something that took her mother by surprise, as it was a rare occurrence these days.

"Okay. I'll try not to," Blu said. They walked the remaining distance up their driveway in silence until they were steps away from the front door.

"Mom, is Gigi my grandma?"

Blu felt her whole body tense up at the question. "No, sweetie, Gigi is not your grandma. Why do you ask that?"

"Claire went to visit her grandma in Ohio last week. They baked cookies and she let her hand out the Bingo cards to the people in the rec hall there. Claire said that it was lots of fun, and I just wanted to know why I couldn't maybe do that with Gigi." She glanced at her Mom as if a new thought had just occurred to her. "Or whoever my grandma is. Mom, who is my grandma?" She had put her hands on her hips as she stood in front of the door. "And why don't we ever go to visit her?"

Now Blu had a headache. The timing of the questions struck her as incredibly ironic, as if a sign of her worst fears coming true. Don't think like that, Blu. She's just asking normal questions that any kid would ask sooner or later.

"Honey, Gigi is kind of like a grandma to you. I'm sure that she would be delighted to think of you as a grandchild because she doesn't have any of her own, you know." Blu was making a mental note to pull Gigi aside to talk to her about this latest line of questioning from Jemma before the child caught her totally off guard. Blu looked at Jemma, who was staring at her as if she was thinking hard about something else as she entered their house.

"That's fine. I'll ask Gigi to bake cookies with me when she gets here, but I want to know about my real grandma."

Blu knew that Jemma wasn't just going to let this go. Gone were the days when any answer would satisfy the inquisitive nature of the child. Now she'd just become completely headstrong, incapable of letting anything go without a fight. She takes after me. Blu couldn't help but smile, even though her head was now pounding trying to find a solution that would stop her daughter from asking more questions. She knew that the questions were only going to keep coming as Jemma got older, so she might as well start thinking about how much she was going to tell her about Blu's mother—about the past that was starting to catch up with her now. She could feel the sense of foreboding deep in her bones.

Jemma turned to look at her before heading to change for the beach. "Mom, are you okay?"

"Yes, I'm fine."

"Well, you look kinda funny." But Jemma wasn't laughing.

She'd always been very sensitive, a quality that Blu found incredibly perplexing. She didn't think she'd done anything special in raising her to be that way, so it must have been something she was born with. A baby fully tuned into the chaos of her environment—God, Blu hoped that wasn't true, that the bad things happening around an infant stayed locked away forever in their not yet fully formed little brains.

"Honey, I'm fine. Now go put your bathing suit on while I pack us a lunch for the beach." Blu really needed a quiet minute to herself, one that she wasn't likely to get for the rest of the day.

Jemma obeyed, scampering up the steps to her room, and Blu poured herself a glass of the wine that she'd opened late last night when she'd returned to the empty house after leaving Chase. She sat down at the small table in the breakfast nook that she loved as much as the one in Victoria's kitchen. She laughed. Before she'd known Arianna, she never knew that breakfast nooks existed or that there was anywhere to ever have a meal except for the dining room table—or more often than not, in her case, the living room coffee table that she'd picked up at a local flea market.

Blu crossed the room to call Jemma upstairs on the intercom.

"Yeah?"

"Hey, sweetie, I was just wondering what you thought about me inviting Chase over for dinner tonight?"

"Is he gonna cook or can we still order pizza?"

Blu had promised this earlier when they'd been planning their beach day. "I'm sure he'd love to join us for pizza. He's been asking me about you, and I know he'd like to see you."

"Yes, I want to see him too. I have to show him the new level I just cleared on the game he bought me. It's so cool."

Blu smiled, thinking about the relationship that had formed between the two. From the moment he'd first met them, years ago with Arianna, a then six-year-old Jemma had taken a strong liking to him. And their relationship had only grown stronger. Blu had a fleeting thought: if only Chase would travel with them to her shows. She trusted him with Jemma, and he'd also do a great job with the schooling piece. She pushed the thought away. Chase wouldn't want to leave his cooking jobs, and she knew that he had a lot scheduled.

She quickly made some sandwiches for herself and Jemma, allowing the child to take her time getting ready as she sat out on the deck sipping her wine. She pulled out her phone to send Chase a quick invitation by text, to which he responded right away. He was doing a luncheon at a party close by and would be able to make if for six o'clock, which was perfect. Blu could spend the whole afternoon with Jemma and then if she was very lucky, and not too tired, Chase would keep Jemma entertained for an hour before dinner so that she could knock out a few things in her workroom.

CHAPTER 7

Blu loved listening to Jemma and Chase playing together while she worked. She smiled as she heard Jemma explaining the latest trick she'd learned about the current level of her video game. Chase had gotten them each the game, himself and her, when it came out a month ago, which really said a lot about his commitment to being in the young girl's life; he rarely had time for video games these days. But he did often make time for Blu's daughter. She smiled as the realization struck her. He definitely was a keeper.

She crossed her workroom to turn on the rock music that always seemed to get her in the zone creatively. She did really intend to get an hour of work in before the three enjoyed some pizza together. The current piece she was working on was going to be fantastic, and Victoria had promised to wear it to the opening of the opera this season. Thinking about the opera for that brief moment made her thoughts turn to Arianna, as they often did as she went about her daily life here in the beach house that her best friend had loved.

She smiled, thinking about that first weekend she and Jemma had spent here with Arianna and how her friend had set her up in this very room with the amazing view of the ocean. Yes, Arianna had been fiercely supportive when it came to Blu's designs. She wondered if Arianna had already been putting the pieces in place for her and Jemma as early as that weekend that they shared. Even during her last days with them all, Arianna, with the help of Douglas, had been arranging everything for them, setting up the gifts that would change the lives of those she loved.

Blu was grateful beyond anything she could express. It was why she'd continued even through the hard times. It was the one thing that had reached through to her in her stubbornness against accepting anything at first. Arianna had taught her the gift of receiving help. She knew that her best friend would be incredibly proud of her for how far she'd come. She would have been Blu's biggest cheerleader; and she still was, in a big way.

Blu turned her attention to the fabric in front of her, determined to get one thing done before dinner.

"Mom…"

She could barely hear Jemma over the loud music, so she crossed the room to turn it down before popping her head out the door. "Jemma, don't yell. Come here, please." Jemma was running down the hall towards her, screaming for her to come in the living room.

"Mom, come quick. You're on TV."

Blu knew instantly what she was going to see; she walked quickly down the hall to sit beside Chase on the sofa. On the TV was one of the big nightly entertainment shows and, sure enough, it was the interview that she'd done at the party a few nights ago. Her heart raced as she watched.

"Mom, you look so great. I can't believe you're—"

"Honey, shh. I wanna hear this, okay?"

Jemma nodded as she went back to the game that had been paused in her hand.

Blu felt Chase's hand on her leg as she sat transfixed looking at the picture of herself on the television in front of them. Oh my God. This is happening.

Chase leaned over to kiss her cheek, whispering in her ear. "Babe, you look amazing on the big screen." He laughed, clearly having fun with Blu's moment in the spotlight.

They watched the quick interview, and the reporter then spoke a few more words about how successful Blu's show had been and that she was definitely the next hot designer to watch out for. The piece closed with the details of Blu's website and where to go for more information on her latest designs.

"I hope your website is going to be able to handle the traffic from this. Have you given your web guy a heads up on everything that's been going on?" Chase said.

Blu had finally spent the time before Fashion Week to

hire someone to do her website and work on her online presence, but she really didn't know that much about it. Her assistant Kate, whom she trusted with the details of her business, had been handling all of that stuff.

"Nah, I'm sure it will be fine," Blu said, barely paying attention because her mind was spinning.

"No, seriously. You're probably going to need to increase your bandwidth," Chase continued. "It happened to me last year when I was interviewed for a news segment, and that was just here in San Diego. My website traffic exploded and the whole thing was down for a good twenty-four hours."

"Okay, I'll send a note to Kate. She's the one who's been dealing with the website guy." Blu really wasn't very technical at all, and most of the stuff regarding her site she didn't pay much attention to. She was more concerned with how the pictures of the pieces showed online and the overall design of the site, which she'd been quite pleased with. She sent a quick text off to Kate, who replied right away that she was on top of it.

Blu sat back down on the sofa next to Chase. Jemma had gone upstairs to phone Claire, so they had a few minutes alone together. Blu felt herself shaking and was trying to hold it together.

Chase reached out to pull her in next to him. "Babe, why do you look so worried? I'm sure that Kate's going to take care of everything. I didn't bring it up to freak you out." He was teasing her, with no idea of what was really bothering her.

"I know. It's not that." She wondered how much she should tell him, how much she needed to tell him.

"Then what is it? I thought your interview was great. You looked a little surprised—towards the end when she was asking you about your family—but other than that I thought you looked completely natural—and sexy," he added, rubbing his hand on her thigh and grinning mischievously.

But Blu was not in the mood for teasing, and she knew there was no hiding how she was feeling. She'd have to talk to Chase about her fears. Not everything, but she'd tell him about her past. She was shaking just thinking about it. It wasn't anything that she ever talked about, and it would be a big step for her. She let herself relax in his arms, her head falling back against his chest, always so strong and available to her. She turned slightly in his arms to give him a kiss on the lips before sitting up.

"I need to talk to you—to tell you some things." She was finding it hard to look him in the eye, but his silent nod and quick kiss was all the encouragement she needed.

"Shall we order the pizza then? I'll hang with Jemma so you can get back to your work for a little while before she goes to bed, and then I will be all yours." He leaned over to kiss the tip of her nose. "Hey, whatever it is that's bothering you—it's going to be okay. I promise."

She was a lucky woman. Chase was busting down the thick walls of distrust around her, one by one. And with each step forward, though not easy, and certainly scary for her, she was marking things off on the list inside her head. He'd certainly been the first guy in a long time at all worthy of her mental checklist.

She offered him a slight smile in response, but inside she was completely stressed out thinking about the conversation to come.

CHAPTER 8

Blu sat waiting for Chase on the sofa, as he went to refill their glasses of wine. She pulled the blanket tight around her, the night ocean breeze blowing cool air in through the windows. A welcome chill to help clear her head.

Jemma had gone to bed after they'd finished their pizza, overtired from the lack of sleep the night before. Blu had tried to work for a bit while Chase and Jemma watched a movie, but she wasn't in the right head space. Finally she'd given up, sitting in her corner chair of the workroom with a glass of wine, attempting to put her jumbled thoughts together about everything that was happening.

Why is it that I always expect the worst possible thing to happen? She smiled, despite the grim nature of the question, because she did know the answer. She'd learned some hard lessons in her life, one of which was that really crappy things seemed to happen to her. And good things have happened too. It was Arianna's voice in her head now. And it was true. A lot of good things had happened to her lately—good things were happening, even now.

She glanced up as Chase entered the living room with the wine; she thought that his timing was impeccable, as always. A gentle reminder of those best things.

"Here you go, darling. I opened another bottle for us."

Blu smiled as she took the glass of Chianti from him, thinking that he must have an idea that they were in for a good long chat. It would feel good to get some of these things out in the open with Chase. She'd shared hardly anything with him about her background, while she had already met his parents, who lived nearby up the coast a bit.

She'd known, early on, that Chase had come from a wealthy upbringing, and one of the things that intrigued her the most was the fact that he worked so hard. She'd guessed that he wouldn't have had to make that choice, but he had a passion for food and cooking, and when he expressed his interest in culinary school, his parents fully supported it. So Blu knew that she would like them, that they wouldn't be the pretentious type, and she'd been right about that. They were very lovely and welcoming to both Blu and Jemma when they'd shared a meal at their lavish home a few months ago. She instantly liked them, and seeing how Chase interacted with them made her fall for him that much more.

"Come here." Chase took the glass out of her hand

and pulled her to him on the sofa. “You look like you could use a big hug.”

She did. She welcomed his embrace and let him hold her to him tightly as she finally released the tears that she’d been holding in for the past few hours. He just held her tightly, stroking her hair and letting her cry. She’d never been this vulnerable with him before, and rarely with anyone, really. She couldn’t remember the last time that she’d cried, and certainly not in front of someone this way.

“Blu, what’s wrong? Maybe I can help you if you tell me about it.”

She knew that he must be pretty confused. She would be, looking at someone who seemed to be on the brink of major success yet completely falling apart at the seams. She took a deep breath, pulling herself out of his embrace to sit up and take a big sip from her wine.

“Chase, I need to tell you some things about my past.”

He was nodding for her to continue as he took her hand in his.

“I—I’ve been on my own for a long time. Since I was sixteen.”

“Okay.” He waited for her to continue.

“My home life sucked, really. It was nothing like yours—like Ari’s. Pretty much you could say that I came from the complete opposite side of the tracks in terms of how I grew up.” She had joked about growing up in a trailer park before with Chase, so she didn't think it would come as a total surprise.

"Okay. You know that none of that matters to me, in terms of the kind of person you are, right?"

"Yes, I do know that." She smiled. She knew that Chase couldn't care less whether or not she came from wealth. He had proven time and time again that he wasn't like that. He was the kind of person who had friends that were millionaires and also had best buddies who were street performing surfers with not a care in the world when it came to financial success.

She took another sip of her wine, getting up the courage needed to just tell him everything. Well, not everything. But a lot more than what he did know about her. "So when I joked about being trailer trash, I really did grow up in a trailer park and—"

"You are not trailer trash. Far from it, Blu." She noticed a look pass across Chase's face as he interrupted her.

"Okay, well, that's how I grew up and, stereotypical as it sounds, my mom was an addict with a lowlife live-in boyfriend that—that used to abuse me." She cast down her eyes to avoid looking Chase in the eye.

His eyes narrowed and she saw his whole body flinch in response to the fist he was clenching in obvious frustration. "What did he do to you?"

There was no mistaking the pain in his eyes and the anger in his body over the story she had begun to tell.

"My mom was with him since I was around ten years old." God, how is that my mom could really have stayed with him all those years? "At first it started with his punishments. He'd use a belt, or sometimes he'd just haul off and hit me with his fist if he was drunk enough. He was out of control, really. And high most often. They both were. God, I hated them both so much."

Chase reached over to pull her towards him, but not before she'd seen his eyes tearing up. "Honey, did he—did he do anything else to you?"

Her face was wet with tears as she nodded, burying her head in the comfort of Chase's chest, his arms hugging tight.

"God, Blu. I'm so sorry that happened to you." They both cried silently, and Blu thought that she'd never felt so close to another person in her life. Finally, after a few moments, she pulled herself up again, disengaging from his arms to reach for her wine.

"That's how I got my name." She usually told people that her nickname came from being such a tomboy that she was always turning up to school with scrapes and bruises, but the truth was that every bruise and mark on her body came from that monster Harold in her home—in their piece-of-crap trailer where there was never any place to escape his foul moods. And her mom was too strung out on drugs to ever care or do a damn thing about it.

Chase let the silence fill the space between them for a

moment as he held her hand and seemed to be gathering his thoughts. Blu's tears had dried up and she felt as though a big weight had been lifted off her shoulders. Finally she felt a sense of freedom with this man who'd had so much patience for her over these past few months.

Chase took her face gently in his hands, tilting her head until she had no choice but to meet his steady gaze. "I want you to know two things beyond a shadow of a doubt." Blu nodded her head, trusting him more than she ever had up until this point.

He continued. "The first is that you didn't deserve any of what happened to you growing up. You do know that, don't you?"

Blu nodded her head in response; she did know it. She'd worked for many years to recognize that fact and was determined to be as healthy a role model for Jemma as she could be; and that included teaching her what it meant to have self-respect, to believe that she deserved only the best things in life.

"The second thing is that I want you to know how much I love you."

Blu was shocked that her eyes were brimming with tears again as she looked at him. Such sweet words coming from this man that she loved. And she did love him. She fully realized it in this moment. She looked up at him, her heart filled and open, maybe for the first time in her life.

"I mean that, Blu. I'm not going anywhere. I'm here

for the long haul with you—with you and Jemma."

She put her arms around his neck and kissed him deeply, willing her lips to speak the depths of emotion that were welling up inside her. She pulled away for a moment, looking into his eyes as she gathered what felt like courage, but knowing there was no need for anything other than the truth of her feelings.

"I love you too, Chase Parker." She grinned widely when she saw the look of surprise on his face. "Oh, stop, silly. You know I've loved you from the moment I first laid eyes on you."

"Is that so?" He teased her as they got comfortable lying on the sofa together, with more conversation ahead.

Blu opened up to him that night, telling him just how bad it had gotten and how she finally left for good and had been on her own ever since. She shared with him her fears about the publicity and how it was bringing up so much dread that she'd be hearing from her mom after all these years.

He would protect her, he said, and there was nothing that her mom or Harold could do to her, but she wasn't convinced. She had Jemma to think about, and when Chase started asking questions about that time in her life—when she'd had Jemma and who the father was—she'd asked him if they could save that conversation for another time. The conversation that night had taken a lot out of both of them, and they'd turned a major corner in their relationship. For that, Blu was incredibly grateful and allowed herself to let the fears go, if only for the night.

CHAPTER 9

Blu sat in the kitchen drinking a cup of coffee and feeling blissfully happy after the night she'd shared with Chase. It was the first time that she'd allowed him to sleep over, and that was only after multiple promises that he would sneak out early before Jemma was awake. It was the first time that she'd really let him in emotionally as well and it was this, more than the physical, that was causing her to feel so content and connected to him.

She was glad to be up early because there were still a few things to be done before Gigi and Douglas arrived late morning. Her housekeeper, Maria, was coming in early to make sure that all the bedrooms were ready, for the couple and for Lia, who would be arriving later in the day. It would be nice to have a house full of people there again, and Jemma was beside herself with excitement. Blu wanted to get a bit of work done because she knew that the rest of the weekend would be full of chats, drinks, and walks on the beach. Chase had promised that he'd return later that afternoon to cook them all a nice dinner.

Blu and Jemma were sitting outside on the deck when Gigi and Douglas pulled up the driveway in the car that Blu had sent to pick them up. Jemma raced over with Blu following behind and laughing at the child's excitement to be reunited with the people who loved her so much. All the family we need, baby girl, is gonna be right here with us.

"Jemma, give them a moment to get out of the car, silly." Blu laughed as Jemma pulled Gigi out the door by her hand.

"Bella, look at you, sweet girl. You've grown so tall." Gigi was hugging Jemma to her; Douglas came around to get his big hug from the young girl.

"That she has indeed," he said, tousling her hair. "I hope that you have a lot of fun things planned for us this weekend."

"I do," Jemma said, grabbing him by the hand. "I can't wait to show you the special spot that Mom and I discovered on the beach."

"Jemma, give them a minute to come inside and get settled. I'm sure there'll be plenty of time to go to the beach," Blu said as she crossed over to give her friends big hugs. "It's so good to see you both."

"And you." Gigi took a step back, scrutinizing Blu for a moment." And why do you look like the cat who swallowed the canary?" She laughed.

Oh God, is it really that obvious? Blu felt her cheeks

grow hot as she thought about the night she'd shared with Chase.

"Silly. Nothing to tell here." From behind Jemma's back Blu mouthed the words "we'll talk later" and winked at her friend.

A few hours later Blu sat outside sipping a glass of wine with both Gigi and Lia, who'd arrived as well, while Jemma enjoyed a walk on the beach with Douglas.

"Finally, some much needed girl talk," Lia said, laughing.

"Yes, don't think I forgot what you alluded to earlier," Gigi said, winking at Blu.

Blu laughed at Lia's quirked eyebrow and funny expression.

"Do tell," Lia said.

"I assume it has something to do with that handsome chef of yours?" Gigi smiled. "And the fact that I've caught you yawning every other time I've looked at you since I got here. Did someone keep you up last night?"

Blu laughed and filled her friends in on the short version of the events of the night before, leaving out the details of both their intense conversation and the intensity of their lovemaking. She was no prude, but for the first time she felt it was important to keep some things just between her and Chase, to give their relationship a certain amount of respect that she'd never allowed in a relationship before.

It wasn't that Gigi and Lia didn't know about her tough upbringing. They did know pretty much everything that she'd shared with Chase, as did Douglas. She'd long since felt comfortable confiding in them; after Arianna died she went through some tough times that required some therapy and a lot of processing when it came to the issues of her past.

The sound of the sliding door interrupted the conversation taking place among the three women. Blu turned around to see Chase making his way to them, dressed in his chef's uniform and looking more handsome than ever.

"Speak of the devil," Blu teased, grinning broadly.

"Oh, is that so?" Chase winked at Lia and Gigi as he bent down to give Blu a quick kiss on the lips. "I certainly hope that you're not telling all our secrets." He laughed.

"No, no secrets." Blu smiled and reached her hand around his waist. "How was your day?"

"My day has been great, and is about to get even better as I settle into the kitchen to prepare you all a feast for this evening."

"Really, Chase. I hope you know that you don't have to do that." Lia was quick to jump in, voicing a concern that she'd expressed to Blu earlier.

"Ah, but I love to cook for my friends. And I know that you know all about that," he directed towards Lia, who was laughing and nodding in agreement.

"Fair enough." Lia said.

Blu smiled at the exchange, because she knew that Lia was exactly the same way when it came to cooking for those she loved. How lucky had she gotten to have two incredible chefs in her life?

"You will tell me if you'd like some help?" Lia asked Chase.

"Yes, I will. And, in fact, I would love to do some cooking with you at some point while you're here. I have an event coming up that will be Italian cuisine, and I'd love to impress them with some authentic Tuscan recipes."

Lia was nodding her head enthusiastically.

"But not for tonight. Tonight I work and you relax out here with your friends."

Blu caught a glimpse of her friends through the kitchen window, sitting around the table with Jemma, enjoying the food that Chase had prepared for them. Her life felt pretty complete. She had an amazing boyfriend, a loving daughter, and the most wonderful friends anyone could ask for. Her career was about to take off in a way that she never could have imagined. Yes, life was good and she was finally allowing herself the chance to enjoy what she'd worked so hard for. *Everything that Arianna wanted for me.*

She heard the tone signaling a text and went over to her phone on the counter. It was a note from Kate, telling her that she'd just forwarded an important email to her that had come via the contact page of Blu's website. She pulled up the email and grabbed the bottle of wine that she'd come to retrieve from the fridge, crossing the floor to head back to the patio as she skimmed the email.

Crash! The bottle slipped from her hand as she stood just inside the door, her heart racing. Out of the corner of her eye, she saw Gigi, Lia, and Chase getting up from the table.

"Ah, I'm such a klutz. Gigi, Lia, you two sit and enjoy the sunset." She tried to keep her voice even, to not show the panic she was feeling.

Her eyes locked with Chase's. "Chase, can you come help me with this please?"

He excused himself and got up from the table to join Blu standing amidst the broken glass. He bent down to start picking up the pieces, asking her to get some towels and a broom without stopping to notice what she was sure was a look of terror on her face. When she didn't move from her spot, he looked at her to speak again.

"Blu, what is it? Your face is as white as a ghost. Are you okay, darling?" She saw a look of worry cross his face as she shook her head to indicate that she was not, in fact, okay.

Chase took her by the arm and stepped over the remaining pieces of glass as he led her to a seat at the breakfast table. "Let me get you a glass of water. What's wrong, baby?" He looked really worried now.

"I just got an email." Blu's voice was very quiet as she

lay down her phone in front of them so they could both see it to read.

Dear Angela, (or I see that you're going by Blu now)

I know this might catch you by surprise, but I've been wanting to find you for awhile now…looking for you with no luck. I saw you on TV the other night. I'm so amazed and proud of your success.

It's hard to write this in an e-mail. There's so much to say. I'll try my best in the hopes that you'll agree to talk to me. To let me see you and Jessica. I'm sober now and Harold is no longer in my life. I've really changed, Blu, and I'd like a chance to prove that to you.

I know you might need a little time to think about all this but I'm coming to California, trusting that you'll find it in your heart to forgive me. For what it's worth, I want you to know that I don't hold anything in the past against you. I only want to move forward.

Can you please give me a chance?

Linda (your mother)

CHAPTER 10

Finally Blu was alone with Chase. It had been hard to keep her composure in front of the others once she'd read the email from her mother, but Chase had promised her that he'd stay until everyone had gone to bed so that they could talk. Thank God I have him right now. Thank God I have Chase in my life, period. She was still in a blissful state of shock at the way she had opened up to him, but she couldn't help but think that the timing had been perfect. She needed him now, and she had a feeling that he was going to prove himself worthy of the trust she'd been wrestling with. Tonight she knew that she had to go all in with him. Tell him everything.

She smiled as he crossed the outside deck to where she was sitting, handing her a glass of wine and seating himself next to her. Her phone sat on the small table in front of them and she eyed it with disdain. She'd already reread the email several times and when Chase asked, she brought it up on her phone for him to look at again too.

"So first, I have some obvious questions," Chase said.

Blu nodded. "Yes, the names."

"Right. I take it that your name is not Brenda then?"

Early on in their relationship, when Chase had asked her about her nickname, she'd told him that her real name was Brenda Foster. It had been so many years ago that Blu had changed her name from Angela White that she didn't even think about it any more—well, until recently, that is.

Blu nodded. "Yes, I was born with the name Angela White. And in the email, where she refers to Jessica, she's talking about Jemma."

"Okay." Chase had a quizzical expression on his face, and Blu knew that he was waiting for more from her.

She took a deep breath and a big sip of her wine as she turned in her seat to face him. All in.

After she had finished, she laid her head back against the seat, noticing that her hands were trembling. Chase handed her wine to her and reached to hold her other hand in his. She waited for him to speak, to go over all of the questions that had been answered about that time in her life when Jemma was born. She knew that it had been the one missing piece of the puzzle for him from their conversation the other night, and now he knew everything. She felt the doubt creeping in, almost without being aware of it. Maybe I've made a big mistake in telling him. A huge mistake that I can't take back now. She looked up at him, willing herself to speak.

"Say something." She searched his eyes for answers as to what he was thinking.

Chase set her glass of wine on the table and pulled her

close to him, wrapping his arms around her tightly. Finally he spoke.

"I think you need to talk to Douglas while he's here."

"To get a restraining order?" Blu said.

"Well, maybe. But you need to tell him everything. You need advice that I can't give you."

Blu tilted her head back to look him in the eyes.

"But I'm here for you. Of course I am." He lowered his head to kiss her gently on the lips. "Douglas will know what to do. And you can trust him."

Blu nodded because she knew Chase was right. She almost felt a sense of relief already, for letting out what she'd been keeping to herself for all these years.

She laid her face on his chest again, allowing the few tears that she'd been holding back to fall. She felt his finger gently wiping them away, his other hand rubbing her back.

"I understand why you did what you did."

Blu felt her whole body relax into his, a loud sob of relief escaping her mouth as she clung to him.

"Everything's going to be okay," Chase said.

And Blu believed him in that moment.

Blu found herself laughing at all of the commotion going on in her kitchen, content to just sit back and watch from the small table tucked away from the busyness. Lia was showing Chase a new Tuscan recipe that she'd mastered and one that they'd all be trying later for dinner.

Gigi and Jemma both looked quite determined to make themselves useful as well.

It was a normal occurrence for Blu to see Jemma following around after Chase in the kitchen, constantly asking him what she could stir or chop—carefully, and only under Chase's supervision and with the much less sharp knife that he brought with him just in case the young girl was around to help.

But to see Gigi in there, so eager and fragile in her attempts, made Blu smile. Clearly she had been making a very good effort to cook more since being married, an effort that Blu was sure Douglas appreciated very much.

She smiled as she thought about how lucky she was to have Chase, not just because he was an amazing chef—that was a big bonus, seeing how she didn't really cook any more than Gigi did—but because he was just an amazing guy, period. Watching him joke and laugh now with her friends made her unbelievably happy, and content with her choice to stop pulling away for once in her life. He was a good man and she was lucky to have him. They both were lucky, she thought as she watched him bend down to give Jemma a quick hug of praise for the good work she was doing kneading the dough for the pasta.

It had been a good day, one that had almost made Blu forget her worries. She'd promised Chase that she would try to set everything aside while they all spent the day together. He'd cleared his schedule to be with them, and they'd had a great time at the beach, building sand castles and swimming in the ocean. Gigi and Lia even let Chase give them their first surfing lesson.

But Blu knew that it was time to have a conversation with Douglas. She could see him out on the deck reading a book, and with everyone busy in the kitchen, they'd be able to talk uninterrupted. She quietly let herself out of the kitchen.

"Hi, whatcha reading?"

Douglas smiled and held his book up so that Blu could read the cover. "Oh, just one of my favorite crime novel authors."

"Good book?" Blu asked.

"It is. Well, it's keeping my interest anyways." He winked.

"I think I heard a rumor about you one time," Blu teased.

"Oh, I'm quite sure that there's been many a rumor spread about me, but what are you referring to?" Douglas teased back.

"That maybe one day you might want to write a book?" Gigi had mentioned this to her one time when she was talking about plans for their future retirement.

"Is that so? That wife of mine would love to see me do it, because that would mean that I'd be retired and we'd be lying on a beach somewhere warm." Douglas laughed, but Blu wondered if there was some friction about that topic between the couple.

"So, not seeing retirement in your near future then, I take it," Blu said, hoping that Douglas wouldn't think that she was prying.

"Oh, we'll see. One of us thinks that I work too much." He winked again.

"And one of you isn't quite ready to slow down, I take it?" Blu smiled, enjoying their easy banter.

"On a serious note, Gigi is the one I'd like to see take a break. She's forever working. Doing something or another around the house, looking after me."

Blu thought that he said the last part as if looking after him was a big chore.

"But isn't that what couples do? Look after one another?"

"A valid point, my dear." Douglas grinned. "I guess the real issue is that I want to take care of her—"

"—And she won't let you," Blu cut in.

"Exactly. Gigi does for everyone besides herself. I'd just love for her to take it easy. Heck, we could afford to have someone—a housekeeper, a cook—to keep up the house for us, but she just insists that she wants to do everything herself."

"Hmm." Blu was thoughtful.

"Hmm, what? Am I wrong?" Douglas said.

"No, no, you're not wrong. I was just thinking that I can relate to that. I'm sure Lia can too, actually. I think your problem is just that you are surrounding yourself with very strong, independent women." They both laughed as Douglas nodded his head in agreement.

"Yeah, true. And I love my wife just the way she is. I won't stop working on it, though."

"I wouldn't either if I were you. It sounds like a nice life to me." Blu laughed and then grew quiet for a few moments, wondering how to broach the subject that was on her mind.

"Douglas? I wondered if I might talk to you about some legal questions that I have."

He studied her face for a moment.

She wondered if there was some kind of "friend boundary" that she was crossing, but Chase had seemed quite sure that Douglas would help her, so she was just going to go forward with it.

"Sure. Shall we go for a walk on the beach where we won't get interrupted by little ears?" Douglas said, pointing towards Jemma, who was right on the other side of the door.

"Yes, thank you," Blu said.

CHAPTER 11

Blu tried to calm her nerves as she and Douglas walked along the beach in silence for a few moments. She knew that Chase was right in that she could trust Douglas. That he was the best person to give her advice and help with her situation. She just didn't know how to tell him everything. It was strange to think that after all these years, she was telling her deepest secrets to not one person, but two in only the space of a few days.

"So, what's on your mind?" Douglas broke the silence between them.

"I—I have this problem. And I think I need some help—some legal help, maybe," Blu said tentatively. "Can I ask—I don't know if this is weird—God, it feels weird now."

Douglas stopped to face her. "Let me first say that anything you tell me now—assuming we're talking because you may be hiring me for legal counsel—would be privileged information. And if you end up not hiring me, it still remains confidential—just between us." He smiled at her and Blu could feel herself relaxing a bit.

"Thanks, that makes me feel better, actually. Not that

I don't trust you—as a friend, I mean. I just wouldn't want to put you in a weird situation."

"I understand," Douglas said. "So tell me what's going on and let's see if I can help you with something."

The two walked along, with Blu filling Douglas in about her past and her current fears about how to handle the situation with her mother contacting her. Douglas listened without interrupting, except to clarify bits of information along the way. When she was finished, she again felt as though her burden was getting just that much lighter. Maybe carrying her secrets around had been much heavier than she'd allowed herself to believe.

They turned around to begin walking back towards the house, and Douglas led her over to a large piece of driftwood, asking if he could read the email one more time as they sat down. Blu pulled the email up on her phone and waited for him to finish. He sat for a minute looking thoughtful before he spoke.

"Can I speak to you first as a friend?" he said.

Blu nodded. "Of course."

"You can hire me if that's your choice and I'm sure that there are some things that I can do to help you, in terms of guarding yourself and your property."

"But?"

"But, when I read this email, I don't hear a woman who has any major battle to wage with you. From that and everything that you've told me, I'm just wondering if you should speak with her first, get a chance to know—"

"—Douglas, I don't have any interest in getting to know her," Blu interrupted.

"I was going to say, getting to know what her intentions are. Only you can decide if you want to do something about that relationship, and I get where you're coming from. I'm not suggesting that I don't. It sounds like you have every reason not to believe her, not to trust her. And if you're right, we can cross that bridge when you come to it." He handed her back her phone with the email still pulled up. "As your friend, I'm suggesting that you at least hear what she has to say, maybe see for yourself if you think she's really changed."

Blu felt the sting of trying to hold back sudden tears. The advice was hard to hear. It wasn't what she wanted. She just wanted to fix the situation and disappear from her mother's life again. The thought came quickly, even as she looked towards her home in the distance. I could do it again. She wondered if Douglas really could protect her or if she needed to be more concerned about Jemma. God, I can't lose her.

She knew she'd do it. Take Jemma and run again, if she had to. She'd leave everything behind. No looking back. Even Chase. Blu wiped the tears away as she felt a new resolve within her, one that she wouldn't share with Douglas, or anyone.

"Douglas, she hasn't changed." Blu said this without emotion, as if it were a fact that anyone would know. "I really have no interest in talking to her, in playing this game with her. I left for a reason, and when I made that decision I knew that it would be forever."

He looked at her with a funny smile.

"What?" Blu wasn't holding back her frustration, apparent in her tone.

"Well, it's just that for someone who I know personally has witnessed a lot of changes throughout the years, I'm a little surprised to hear you talking about forever."

Blu questioned him with her eyes.

"I mean, you've seen yourself the changes that people can go through. Maybe your mom is not so different? Anything is possible, you know."

Blu was nodding her head but only to appease him, let him know that she was considering his words even though inside, her only thought was of running.

"You know what I think?" Douglas said.

"What's that?"

"I think maybe you should talk to Lia while she's here."

"You think I should tell all of this to Lia?" Blu was a bit surprised by the suggestion, not that Lia wasn't a friend that she could confide in.

"No, I'm not advising that you should talk to her about everything. You shouldn't. Not yet. But I think you should talk to her about the possibility of seeing—"

Blu glared at him, shaking her head. That is not happening. I am not going to see my mother after all these years.

"Or at least speaking with your mother on the phone," Douglas continued. "Don't you think that Lia might have a unique perspective on all of this?"

"Lia and Ari's situation was nothing like this."

"Hmm."

"Hmm what?"

"Well that's only true if your mother hasn't changed."

Blu looked at him, sure that her disbelief was written all over her face.

"Trust me, she's not changed."

"I don't really get how sure you are about all this, if I'm being honest. People change, Blu. They do." Douglas looked out towards the ocean, and Blu thought she detected something personal in his simple statement.

She had no reason not to listen to him, to trust him. She'd already decided that, when she made the decision to trust him with her secrets.

"You're right. People do change." But not my mother.

They got up to make the walk back towards the house.

"So you'll talk to Lia then?

Blu was lost in her own jumbled thoughts, undecided about how she felt regarding the conversation that she'd had with Douglas.

"Blu?"

"Sorry, what was that?" Blu said.

"You'll talk to her? To Lia?"

Blu nodded. "Yeah, I will." She sighed. She really just wanted this all to be done very soon. "I'll see how the rest of the day goes but maybe we can catch a chat in the morning." She knew that Lia would probably still have a bit of jet lag, so the possibility that she could catch her early over coffee was a good one.

Douglas stopped just short of the steps leading up to Blu's house. "To be clear, I will help you. Whatever you decide. I want to be sure that you know that."

Blu smiled, putting her hand on his arm. "I do know that, Douglas. And I appreciate you so much. Your advice means everything to me. It does." She leaned over to give him a quick kiss on the cheek, recognizing that he had become a sort of father figure to her—which was actually very nice, because it had been something completely missing from her life.

They smiled at one another, content that everything was okay for now, as they made their way up the stairs to the dinner that they could smell on the table.

CHAPTER 12

Blu woke up and stared at the alarm clock with suspicion. What the heck time is it? She'd been tossing and turning all night with way too much on her mind and finally, with no expectation that she'd wake up early after all, must have fallen asleep. But the clock said five fifteen, and she could smell the brewed coffee from downstairs, suspecting it would be Lia up this early as Blu had predicted.

She pulled the covers tighter, deciding to give herself just five more minutes in bed before facing the reality of her current worries. Her thoughts turned towards last night and how wonderful it felt seeing Jemma laughing and playing with everyone. It was great having all her friends here, and Blu vowed that they'd organize a future meet-up again before the crew dispersed, maybe in Italy. And maybe she'd take Chase. She smiled at the idea, knowing that he'd traveled a bit, but never to Italy, and that it was very high on his list of places he'd like to visit.

Thinking about last night reminded her again of her

talk with Douglas and the promise she'd made to speak with Lia. She sighed, having no idea how it would go or what Lia would think about her mother contacting her. Would she be able to be objective about the whole thing? No use lying in bed wondering about it, Blu thought as she got up to make her move downstairs.

The kitchen windows were open and the morning breeze coming in was just the right temperature for thick robes and coffee. Blu pulled her robe tighter around her, then reached for a coffee cup as she noticed Lia sitting outside watching the ocean.

The sight of her nearly took her breath away. It was impossible not to be reminded of Arianna whenever Blu looked at Lia. The resemblance was really amazing, and whenever Blu saw Lia now, she reminded her so much of the best friend that she'd lost. Not that it was bad. It wasn't.

It had been rough going, especially, that first year after Arianna died. She'd had a hard time herself, and Jemma, being pretty young, cried herself to sleep many nights, not understanding where her friend had gone. They'd both gone through a lot, with the help of a good therapist and their friends; things were much better, and it seemed they all had a healthy perspective on the things that Arianna had brought to their lives, in terms of the memories and the legacy she'd left to each of them.

Blu poured her coffee and noticed Lia motioning to

her from outside.

"Good morning, early bird," Blu said as she walked out onto the deck to sit opposite her friend at the table.

"I know. I've been up since four o'clock, actually. Jet lag does it to me every time." She laughed. "How 'bout you? Why are you up so early? Normal for you?"

Blu nodded her head. "At least lately it seems to be. My schedule's been a little messed up too, I guess. Plus I've not really been sleeping very well."

Lia looked at her, brow furrowed. "Are you okay? Something you wanna talk about?"

"I do want to talk you, yes. But first I want to hear all about you. Before the others get up, and by others I mean Jemma wanting all of your attention." The two women laughed.

"Oh, it's so good to be around her. To be here. I miss you all a lot."

Blu knew that she meant it but also knew that Lia seemed more content than she'd ever seen her, something she'd noticed even in the short time since her arrival.

"Well, you certainly do seem very happy." Blu said. "I assume everything is going well with the restaurant and with Antonio?"

"Yes, Carlo and I are like a well-oiled machine at Thyme. The restaurant practically runs itself, we've got such great help right now." She laughed. "Well, maybe that's an exaggeration, but Sofia has become our manager now that she's out of school, and she's got a wonderful staff working for us right now. I couldn't be more pleased."

"That's so great to hear. Just talking about it is making me miss those delicious Italian feasts." She laughed. "Not that last night wasn't great—and by the way, that dish was fantastic. I think Chase was well pleased with himself, don't you?" Blu smiled.

"I have to say, Blu. I really like that man of yours. He's a keeper." She looked at Blu with a question on her face. "I hope you do realize that?"

Blu laughed, feeling her face grow a bit hot. "I do, yes. As of lately, there's nothing I want more than to make this relationship work with him. I think it's worth it."

"Well worth it." Lia said. "And he adores you. I can tell."

"Speaking of adoring boyfriends…" Blu laughed. "How's everything between you and Antonio?"

Lia's face seemed to light up across from her at the mere mention of Antonio's name. "He's so great. We're so great, actually. Something I wasn't ever sure that I'd be saying."

Blu nodded, remembering the rocky start the two had had to go through after their initial reunion in Italy a few years earlier.

"And what exactly do you mean by so great?" Blu teased with a wink. "Is there talk of finally moving into the vineyard villa with him? I can't believe that you've been keeping two places for this long."

"Yes, we've been talking, in fact. Up until now, it made sense to keep my place, which is so close to the restaurant, but lately I've not been going in every day; and really, Antonio's only a short drive away. And, well—"

"Spill it. Are you getting ready to tell me what I think you are? Are we getting wedding invitations soon?" Blu grinned broadly at her friend.

Lia blushed, nodding her head. "It's not official yet so I've not told the others—or anyone really—but yes, I think there's a good chance that you'll be invited to a wedding at the vineyard—maybe late summer or early fall—so do keep that in mind when it comes to your travel plans."

Blu got up to come around the table and hug her friend, genuinely very pleased for her. "Wait." She released Lia from her hug, stepping back a bit. "You are going to let me make your dress, aren't you?"

Lia's eyes filled with tears. "Oh, I was hoping you'd say that. Yes. Yes, please. And a flower girl dress for Jemma, but let's not get ahead of ourselves." Lia laughed.

"Well, this is just the best news—and let's try to at least sneak away at some point while you're here to look at some magazines and do some sketching."

Lia nodded, still looking a bit overcome by emotion. "That sounds wonderful."

Blu was looking at Lia thoughtfully. She really couldn't believe how far Lia had come since she'd met her—really since after Arianna's death. If Lia had gone through everything she'd gone through and was, in fact, getting her happy ending, then Blu had to believe that she'd make it through this rough patch too.

"I'm just so happy for you, Lia." And Blu meant it with every ounce of her being. "And God, Ari would be so pleased. You do know that, right?"

Lia nodded, fresh tears springing to her eyes. "Not a day goes by that Antonio and I don't remember that it was Ari that brought us back together after so many years—and so many mistakes."

Blu nodded in recognition of the mistakes Lia referred to. She knew Lia's story and the secrets that had been kept for a long time. But she also knew the rest of the story, which was all about what was possible after making the decision to move on.

Blu hugged her friend again before she went back to sit across from her at the table.

"Okay, enough about me." Lia said wiping her eyes one last time. "What did you want to talk about?"

CHAPTER 13

Blu laughed to herself at the irony of Lia's statement, because what they'd been talking about for the last several minutes spoke exactly to Blu's questions about taking chances, forgiveness, and moving on from past mistakes.

"So I was talking to Douglas yesterday about some issues—or potential issues—that I could be having." Blu saw the look on her friend's face and hurried to ease her concern. "Everything's okay, so no need to worry. Well, at least I think everything will be okay—eventually."

Lia was nodding her head. "Go on."

"So anyways, I've recently been contacted by my mother—right after that interview with me came out. I can't say that I was really shocked by it, but I'm not happy and I'm trying to figure out a way to keep my mother away, basically; thus my asking Douglas for advice as to what I could do legally." Lia was listening intently, nodding her head.

Blu had shared with Lia the rough childhood that she'd had. She knew most of the bits about her mother and the drugs and even the stuff about Harold and the abuse. She knew almost everything; and she certainly knew how Blu felt about the woman that she never even referred to except when something about her past happened to come up in conversation. Even in cases like that, she tried very hard to avoid the subject.

"So Douglas suggested that I should talk to you about it before I made any decisions. And by decisions, I mean keeping my mother away from me and Jemma at all costs." Blu was frustrated again just talking about it.

"He thought that you should talk to me?" Lia looked confused, like she hadn't quite made the connection yet, which made sense because she was probably thinking about Blu's mother as the strung-out druggie that Blu had described to her so many times.

"Yeah, well, the thing is, this email that my mom sent talked about how much she had changed. That she wanted another chance, basically, to make things right between us. I dunno. I mean, I'm not really buying it, but Douglas seems to think that it might be worth considering speaking with her, at least."

Lia was nodding her head again. "And he thinks that I might be able to offer a perspective as someone who also took a chance reaching out to my daughter."

"Exactly. Oh, here, let me just read it to you." Blu brought it up on her phone and mentally reminded herself to change the names as she read it. When she was done reading, the two sat in silence for a few seconds until Lia seemed ready to voice her opinion.

"Okay, I can understand why Douglas didn't want to do anything too quickly."

Blu nodded. She did understand that too, even though she was freaking out and wanted the whole thing over with right away, as it was really causing her a lot of stress.

"And you know that we all—I'm sure I can speak for Gigi too—we all only care about your happiness—and Jemma's, of course—what might be best for you."

Blu nodded, but in her head she was thinking about all the things that Lia didn't know.

"So, I can be totally honest with you about what I think?" Lia asked, treading carefully.

"Yes, of course."

"What I heard you read to me—that email from your mother—sounds very genuine. Or at least like it's coming from someone who you might want to at least listen to. I mean, is there any harm in talking to her on the phone? You just have to remind yourself that ultimately it will be your decision as to how you go forward—if you decide to do that."

Blu nodded, but inside she only had more confusion to wade through.

"But really…It's so hard for me to imagine that's she's changed. And also, is it a coincidence that she's contacting me now after seeing that I've had some success in my life?" Blu was daring her friend to disagree with her.

"You could be right about that." Lia's voice grew just a bit quieter as if to make a point. "I'm sure Ari had some of those same concerns about me when I first contacted her."

Blu nodded because she knew it was true. But Arianna had also been dying. It was different. That was what Blu told herself when doubts about her stance crept in. What if my mom really has changed? Would that be amazing? What would it mean for Jemma, though? Blu just couldn't fathom any of this working out okay. She sighed.

"You're right, she did," Blu said in response to Lia's comment about Arianna's doubts, of which Blu had had firsthand knowledge. It had worked out well for Arianna and Lia. There was no doubt about that.

"I mean, can you imagine giving her a chance?" Lia asked carefully. "I'll bet that you'd have a pretty good idea after a first meeting—" Blu instinctively cringed at the thought of seeing her mom.

"—or even an initial phone conversation," Lia continued. "Maybe she really has changed. Wouldn't it be kind of amazing for you—and for Jemma to be able to know her grandma? "

"I don't know. That's the part that's making me the most stressed, if I'm being honest. I just don't want anything negative in Jemma's life, ya know?"

Lia nodded. "Yes, I can understand that. But she is

getting old enough to understand more now. I guess you need to look at the worst-case scenario, and think about what that would be like for both you and Jemma. And I'm guessing that if that occurred—that if anything got ugly—Douglas would be able to help you with some of that, legally, I mean."

"Yes, I think he could help me to get a restraining order, and I could hire security if I needed to." But in her head she was reminded that that really wasn't the worst thing that could happen, and she felt her initial resolve rising up again inside her.

"Well, I just know how grateful I was to Ari for giving me that second chance. I don't need to tell you how much it changed my life—how much I believe that it changed both of our lives."

"Yes, I do understand that."

"And the fact that I do have a granddaughter out there somewhere—you have no idea how that feels. I know it's not exactly the same, because it does sound like your mother has seen Jemma at least, that they knew each other?"

Blu thought carefully about how to respond.

"Well, not really. I mean, I left with Jemma when she was a baby. She doesn't remember anything about my mother."

"Oh." Lia grew quiet.

"What, Lia?"

"Well, I'm just wondering what is the best thing for

Jemma. Do you wonder that?"

"Yes, of course I do." Blu didn't mean to sound as frustrated as she was feeling, but it was hard to hold it back. "Just this past week, in fact, Jemma was asking about her grandmother."

Lia raised an eyebrow as Blu continued.

"Yeah, I know. Very weird timing considering she'd never brought it up before." Blu laughed despite her discomfort. "She actually asked me if Gigi was her grandma."

Lia laughed. "That's sweet; did you tell Gigi?"

"No, I've not really had a chance to yet, but I told Jemma that I'm sure Gigi would be flattered to act as her honorary grandma."

"Does this have anything to do with Jemma begging Gigi to make cookies with her the other day?"

Blu burst into laughter. "Yes, in fact it does. I didn't have the heart to tell Jemma that we'd be better off getting a box mix from the store."

"So aside from preferring a grandmother who can bake, it sounds like the timing of this could be very good. That's if you feel comfortable."

"About them meeting, ya mean? Yeah, I'd say that's a big if," Blu said.

"Are you willing to at least entertain the idea?" Lia asked.

Blu thought about this carefully before responding. "Yes, I suppose that I should consider it, although I have to be honest and say that every part of me is leaning towards trying to block her from seeing either of us. I'm just not sure how to go about that. Or if there's a possibility of it backfiring on me, which could be pretty bad." She felt exhausted thinking about it now. She really needed for it to be done so that she could get on with her life and all of the work that she had coming up.

Lia smiled at her and reached out her hand to touch her arm across the table. "I'm sure you'll make the decision that is best for you—and Jemma."

"I hope so," Blu said. "I do appreciate your insight. It's been very interesting to hear another perspective on it all."

"Well, all I can say is that I can't stress enough how happy I am that I took that chance years ago to connect with Ari. Had I not done that—and believe me, there were plenty of days that I didn't think that I had the courage to do it—but had I not done it, my life wouldn't be half the life I have today. And I'm not talking at all about the material things that Ari gave me."

Blu nodded, understanding exactly what Lia meant.

CHAPTER 14

Blu spent the next few days in a busy whirlwind of entertaining her guests and getting some much-needed work done. Gigi, Douglas, and Lia were more than willing to spend a lot of time with Jemma, which Blu thought was good for her daughter as well. So she willingly used some of that time to make some decent progress on her new collection of designs. It was easy to push any thoughts about her mother and the email out of the way for now. She'd deal with it tomorrow after her guests left.

Blu was sad to think about them leaving. It had been so nice having a house full of people, and she knew that it would seem very quiet to both her and Jemma once they'd all left. She made a mental note to ask Jemma if she wanted to invite Claire over for a night, and she'd invite Chase over for dinner too.

She grinned, thinking about Chase and wondering when they might have the chance to spend the night together again. It had been difficult to not spend any real time alone together since that first night right before her guests had arrived. But she wouldn't have traded the past week for anything. He'd been so wonderful spending all of his free time with her and her friends. She loved it that they'd gotten a chance to really get to know him, and she knew that they all thought a great deal of him, fully giving her their blessing, if that was what she was asking for.

"Mom—" Blu's thoughts were interrupted by Jemma's running into the kitchen and hurling something at her. "Mom, put this on and come out on the deck with us."

Blu looked at the Mickey Mouse ears in her hand and smiled. They'd just gotten back from Disneyland and Jemma had had the best time—they all had.

"Mom, hurry. Douglas is setting the camera up to take the picture of all of us."

Blu put the ears on and headed out to the deck, where everyone else was already assembled in a wonderful close huddle of Disney celebration—all with their ears on, all with big grins. Blu took her place next to Chase and smiled, waiting for the timed click of the camera that Douglas had set up on the tripod. This little family of hers. She loved them all so much. She felt tears stinging her eyes.

Jemma grabbed her hand to pull her over to a little corner of the deck.

"Douglas, will you take another picture?" She looked at Blu. "Just you and me, Mom—with our little beach in the background."

Blu couldn't speak for fear of the tears coming that she was trying so desperately to keep inside. She hugged

Jemma close for the picture, laughing at the child's silly poses and instructions for how she wanted Blu to pose with her.

"I will remember this day always," Jemma said in the overly dramatic way that she had when she was trying to be silly, but as Blu looked at her laughing, her sun-bleached hair shining in the remaining light of the day, she knew that it was what she wanted. Above all else. To see Jemma's smile, to create memories for her that would last her lifetime. Blu felt a renewed commitment, a renewed sense that everything was going to be alright. She'd make sure of that.

Blu walked into the kitchen to check on the snack that Maria was preparing for everyone to eat before they all headed off to the airport for their evening flights. "How's it going, Maria? Is everything almost ready?"

"Yes; would you like me to take the food out to the deck?"

"Sure, that would be great. Thanks."

Maria stopped to turn towards Blu on the way to the door. "Did you see the message by the phone?"

"Oh no, I've not had a chance to look yet. Anything important?"

Maria had come to know Blu well; Blu counted on her as the fielder of many phone calls to do a good job of collecting the important details of anything that she felt needed Blu's attention. And Maria rarely let her down in this regard.

"Linda called…"

The simple statement hung in the air as if there was a question mark coming at the end of it.

Maria continued. "She said that she's your mother…"

Blu felt as if she'd been punched in the gut. It wasn't something she was prepared to deal with today. But that's what I get for putting it off all week.

"What did she say?" Blu's voice was quiet.

"She asked that I ask you to phone her back. I wrote the number down on that paper there for you." Maria gestured towards the counter near the phone.

Blu crossed the room to pick up the piece of paper, feeling a bit unsteady suddenly, as if she might pass out.

"Are you okay? You look very pale." Maria had set the tray of food back down on the kitchen table and was heading towards Blu.

Blu let Maria lead her to a chair and took the glass of water that she handed her. Deep breaths. Just take some deep breaths.

"Shall I get someone?" Maria was asking her, a look of real concern on her face by this point.

"Will you—will you get Chase for me, please?"

Maria was nodding her head, making her way to the door.

"And Maria—please don't mention anything to the others. If you could just get them started on their snack, because they'll be leaving soon for the airport."

Maria turned around to pick up the tray of food once

again. "Yes, of course. Don't worry."

Before Maria could get Chase, Lia had slipped into the kitchen.

"Here you are. Are you going to come outside and sit with us for a few minutes before we leave? I'm so sad to—Blu, what's wrong?" Lia quickly crossed over to where Blu was sitting.

Blu imagined that she must really look like she'd seen a ghost. She was desperately trying to hold it together for the remaining minutes before her guests departed, but judging from both Maria's and Lia's reactions to seeing her face, she was doing a very poor job of that.

She tried to smile, and thought about keeping the new information from Lia. She didn't want to say anything that would ruin the great day they'd all just had or end the week on anything other than a good note. But looking at Lia's concerned face, she saw no point in concealing her obvious stress.

"My mom called."

"She did?"

"Yeah, while we were out today. Maria just gave me the message." Blu opened up the folded piece of paper that was still in her hand. "She left her number, asking me to call her back."

"Wow. Are you okay?" Lia asked, eyeing her carefully. "Do you want me to stay a bit longer? Because I could do that, if you think you'd like me to be here with you for some of these things that you need to work out."

Blu shook her head. "No, no, but thank you. I don't want to keep you from Antonio and the restaurant, your amazing life in Italy."

"Are you sure? Because I wouldn't offer if I couldn't do it—if I didn't want to. And I—I know how it is to be feeling alone while in the middle of a crisis. I'd hate for you to feel that way." Blu saw the question in Lia's eyes and she felt the support that her friend offered to her.

"I'll be okay. Really. And I have Chase now, so I'm not alone." Blu smiled. And she realized that she meant it.

"And you have me—all of us—just a phone call away—or I'm sure Gigi and Douglas would stay another day—"

"No, really. I'm going to try to handle this by myself for now—well, with Chase, I mean." It felt good to hear herself saying the words. "It just took me by surprise when Maria gave me the message, but I'm already feeling better about it. I just need to get it over with," Blu said.

"Does that mean that you're going to call her back, then?" Lia asked tentatively.

"Yes, I will do. Tonight, after I've had a chance to get my thoughts together about it."

"And once you've got some peace and quiet in this house again." Lia laughed.

Blu got up from the table, tucking the small piece of paper into the pocket of her jeans. "And on that note, let's head outside to get you a bite of something before you have to leave." She reached over to give Lia a hug before they headed to the door. "And for the record, I'm really sad that it's going to be so quiet here again." She looked her friend in the eye. "I'm really gonna miss you. As will Jemma."

"Me too. But—"

"But we should be expecting our wedding invitations in the mail soon?" Blu whispered in her friend's ear as they opened the door to go outside and join the others.

Lia turned around to wink at Blu as the two women settled in at the table. The others were drinking a last glass of wine and eating the various meats and cheeses that Maria had assembled for them.

Chase leaned over to give Blu a quick kiss on the cheek. "Are you okay?" he whispered in her ear. "Maria told me you needed me, but then you and Lia seemed pretty deep in conversation."

Blu nodded her head, appreciating his steady support next to her. It felt really good to trust someone again. She put her head next to his. "Yeah, I'm okay." And noticing the question in his eyes, "My mother called here while we were out. Fill you in later?"

He nodded and took her hand under the table.

CHAPTER 15

The remaining time with her friends went way too quickly, and before Blu knew it the car that she'd hired was there to pick them up. Jemma was crying in the driveway, tightly hanging on to Lia as if she was never going to see the poor woman again. Blu bent down to whisper in the little girl's ear.

"Honey, we'll see Lia soon. Maybe in Italy." Blu smiled as Jemma looked to Lia to confirm this news.

Lia nodded her head in agreement. "Yes, I propose that our next get-together be at my place."

"Or the vineyard," Gigi chimed in, laughing.

Blu looked at Lia, who shrugged her shoulders, grinning like that cat who'd eaten the canary.

"I don't know what you all are going on about, but Italy sounds like a fine idea to me," Douglas said, as he helped carry the suitcases to the waiting limo.

After a round of hugs and kisses, Blu, Jemma, and Chase stood waving one last time as the car doors shut and their friends drove away.

Chase spoke first. "Shall I make us something for dinner, or does anyone feel like pizza?" He winked at

Jemma.

"Can we, Mom?"

"Yep, seems like a good plan to me. Why don't you go on up and have a shower and get ready for bed?"

Blu wanted just a moment alone with Chase, which Jemma may have sensed because she went straight upstairs without having to be told a second time.

Chase came up behind Blu as she sat on the sofa, rubbing her neck in a way that instantly caused her to relax. God, that feels good. And it made her realize just how tense she'd been lately. He came to sit next to her, taking her hand in his and giving her a quick kiss on the lips.

"Wow, it's been a busy week, huh?" Chase said.

"Yes, it has." She turned to look at him. "Thanks for being around so much. It really means a lot to me."

"Are you kidding? I wouldn't have been able to do without you after that last night we shared together." He leaned in to kiss her deeply.

Blu laughed. "I think we've been having similar thoughts."

"But I thoroughly enjoyed spending time with you all. I really like your friends a lot."

"Really?" Blu was delighted that everything had gone so well. "They like you a lot too." She sighed, remembering that she still had things to take care of.

"So tell me, what's going on with your mother? And

the phone call?"

Blu filled him in on everything, ending with the fact that she'd promised Lia—and herself—that she'd return that call tonight.

"But maybe I'll do it in the morning. I'm pretty tired."

Chase was looking at her with a funny expression on his face.

"Out with it," Blu said.

"I just think you should do it. How 'bout after dinner I'll entertain Jemma with a game or a movie and you go upstairs and just get it over with. Then you'll know once and for all."

Blu nodded her head slowly, knowing he was right.

Blu's heart was racing as she punched the number Maria had written down into her phone. Please don't answer. One ring, two rings…

"Hello."

Blu vaguely recognized the voice on the other end, and the recognition of this fact was startling. She got up from her bed to look out the window as she tried to calm her racing heart.

"Hello?" the woman said a second time.

"Hello—hi." Blu's own voice croaked out after much effort on her part.

"Who is this? Angela? Is that you?"

"Yes, it's—I go by Blu now," she stammered out, willing herself to be calm. She could hear what sounded like a sharp intake of breath on the other end of the phone.

"I—I'm so glad you called me. I really didn't think you were going to when I never heard back. But then I—I didn't know if you got my email. Did you?"

"Yes. I got it." Blu said. "It really surprised me so I—I didn't quite know how to react."

"It's been a long time," her mom said.

Blu was really having a hard time forming her sentences, surprised by her inability to hurl the harsh thoughts that she'd been forming the past few days at her mother, telling her to stay away and leave her and Jemma alone. The words just didn't come.

"What—what do you want?" Blu finally said quietly.

"I—I don't want anything from you. I've wanted to reach out to you over the past few years, but I couldn't—you changed your names and I had no way to find you—but I've thought about you—and Jessica—every day." She stopped talking and then there was silence for several seconds.

"Blu?"

"Yes. I'm here. I—I just don't know what to say." And she didn't. Her mind was going a million miles an hour. She didn't expect her mom's voice to sound so clear.

"I've changed, Blu. I have."

Her mom continued to speak, and the voice Blu heard on the other end of the line only seemed to get stronger with each word.

"I'm here—in San Diego. And I'd really like to see you."

Blu's heart was pounding fast again. She's here. I waited too long to tell her not to bother coming and now what? She wasn't ready for this.

"I—I don't know. I don't think it's a good idea." Blu forced the words out. God, she was really scared now. What was going to happen to her—and Jemma? In her head, she started making a mental checklist of what she needed to do to put her plan into action. This was happening. She'd just have to take Jemma and leave everything—and everyone—behind.

"You need to know that I don't blame you for anything in the past. Blu, I don't want to hurt you—or take Jessica. You don't need to worry about that."

Blu allowed her mind to slow down as she tried to focus on the words being spoken to her. For some reason that she couldn't quite comprehend, there was the beginning of a little bit of hope—or a shred of doubt about everything that she believed to be true about the mother who had lied to her so many times when she was younger. She certainly sounded much different.

"Really?" Blu managed to squeak out. "Are you telling me the truth? Because everything I've ever done, I've done for Jem—Jessica—and I won't stop protecting her now. You need to know that." Blu's voice grew stronger now with every word.

"I do know that. I do," her mom said.

Silence filled the space between them again as Blu tried to think of what to do.

"Please just give me a chance. One meeting. Just with you. I'm only here for a few days and I'd—I'd just like a chance, Blu. That's all. No commitments, no promises. I only want to sit down with you face-to-face. Please." She was pleading, but Blu got the sense that this would be the end of it, that she'd said her piece and the rest was up to Blu.

Blu looked out her window at the infinite waves of the ocean, so vast and magnificent. It always made her think about possibilities. It reminded her of all the hard work that she'd put in downstairs in her workroom, sewing and designing at her table, with the ocean in front of her, urging her to press on toward everything that she'd been dreaming for. It reminded her of being here with Arianna, out on the deck, her friend's smile wide and her laughter loud even as her days were slipping away.

"Blu?" Her mother's voice on the other end of the phone cut into her thoughts and she knew that she had to make a decision.

Blu took a deep breath. "Okay," she said.

CHAPTER 16

Blu looked at Chase over the top of Jemma's head as the two were finishing up a board game that Jemma was obviously winning, by the sounds of her squeals. Blu mouthed the words "we're meeting" to Chase, who raised his eyebrow, then reached for her hand, giving it a gentle squeeze. She was anxious to tell him about how the phone call had gone—how it had felt to be talking to her mother. She watched Chase as he interacted so wonderfully with her daughter. How did I get so lucky with him? Blu thought for about the hundredth time this past week. She'd had no idea when she first started dating him that he would turn out to be such a source of support to her. Well, whoever knew how these things were gonna turn out? She was learning, that was for sure. It definitely seemed to be the theme of the month. To trust.

"I win!" Jemma shouted after her roll of the dice.

Blu and Chase laughed.

"Jemma, be a good winner," Blu said, trying to put on a stern face.

"Oh, I'm a great winner," Jemma laughed, holding her arms above her head to indicate her victory.

"Well, take your winning attitude on upstairs to get ready for bed. You've been yawning this whole time, and I think that you have some sleep to catch up on after the busy week we've had." Blu playfully tapped her on the bottom.

"Okay, mother dear." Jemma gave them both a hug. "Oh, can I go over to Claire's tomorrow? She has a new game she wants to show me."

"Yes, I'm sure that that should be fine. I'll phone Claire's mom in the morning. Good night, kiddo."

After Jemma had left, Chase leaned in to Blu sitting on the couch, giving her a deep kiss. God, how is that I've missed him so much when we've been around each other all week? She found herself wondering if they dared sneak upstairs to her bedroom once Jemma was asleep, just as quickly trying to erase the thought from her mind. She wasn't ready yet for Jemma to catch them in a compromising position—well, not that that should ever happen. But she didn't want to have to explain her relationship to her just yet. She noticed, though, that she no longer had the same fears about Chase disappearing out of Jemma's life—or her own, for that matter. She didn't know exactly what that meant or what it would eventually lead to, but she did believe that Chase was in the picture for the long haul, something that made her very happy.

Chase pulled away and got up. "I'll go get us a glass of

wine." He bent down to give her a quick kiss. "I'm guessing maybe you could use one?"

Blu nodded. "Yes, thanks. I think a glass—or two—might be in order tonight."

Surprisingly, she wasn't feeling as upset as she had been about everything before she'd talked to her mother. She was still very skeptical and guarded about believing her, but she felt stronger about it. And less inclined to run away. As she watched Chase reenter the room with the wine, she didn't know if she really would have had it in her to do that anyways. To leave him. But just as quickly as she had the thought, it was Jemma's face that she saw, and she knew that she could do it—for Jemma. Everything had always been about her, and she needed to continue focusing on the little girl, no matter what else was happening in her life—even Chase.

She took the wine from Chase and, after a big sip, settled back against his chest as he pulled her close.

"God, you feel good in my arms," he whispered in her ear.

She felt his lips on her neck, sending chills up and down her spine. She turned her face to kiss him on the lips. "I do feel good being in your arms." She laughed. "Amazingly so, in fact."

"Is that so," he teased. "So tell me about the phone call."

It felt good to Blu to go over it with Chase. She recounted as much of the conversation as she could remember and told him that she'd be meeting her mom the day after tomorrow in a coffee shop downtown.

"And how are you feeling about this meeting? Nervous?" Chase asked.

Blu thought about the question for a few seconds. "No, I wouldn't say that I'm exactly nervous, although ask me again that morning and it's likely I'll feel different." She laughed. "Oddly, it felt kind of good talking to her. Once we got over the initial awkward moments." She sat up and away from him on the sofa so that they could look at one another. "I mean, none of it was comfortable and I still have so many doubts."

Chase nodded his head.

"For some reason the one thing I did believe was that she wasn't here to take Jemma. But it could be that I believe that because it's hard for me to imagine that she's really clean now. For good, ya know?" She looked at Chase for some reassurance.

"I think you should be able to trust your instinct with her. And you know that you have Douglas to help you, should it come to that."

Blu felt herself tense up. "God, I hope I'm not wrong about this. About seeing her, I mean."

"Well, it makes sense to me, Blu. She's obviously trying, and it will be up to you to decide how authentic you feel she is being."

"Well, I guess I feel that had I not called her back, I was risking her just turning up anyway, ya know? I really need to take my address off that website, now that I'm thinking about it."

She made a mental note to email Katie about that right away. They'd used it for the business address when the website had first gone up, which was ages ago. Things were different now, and she needed to think about Jemma's—about their—safety now that people knew about her brand—about her.

"I think that was the right call. She's obviously pretty desperate to see you, coming out here and all," Chase said.

"I guess I'll find out just what that's all about."

Chase nodded his head in agreement.

"God, I can't believe I'm gonna be seeing my mother." She sighed, wanting it to be over as she realized the nerves were coming now.

Blu took the coffee that Victoria handed her, happy for the chance to catch up with her friend. Victoria and her family had been in Mexico for Spring Break so it had been over a week since they'd spoken. There was a lot to catch her up on.

"Wow, girl. You have had a very eventful week, haven't you?" Victoria said once Blu had given her the shortened version on everything from being in love with Chase to the meeting with her mother tomorrow.

Blu nodded. "Yes, I can't believe all that's happened since I last spoke with you."

"Starting with this little shift in your relationship with Chase." Victoria laughed. "You know that that makes me insanely happy for you, and it sounds like you're doing a great job being open with everything."

"It does feel really huge." Blu could feel her face growing warm.

"What?"

"I don't wanna jinx it." Blu laughed. "But, I dunno. I really feel like maybe he could be the one, ya know."

Victoria grinned. "Of course he could be. And I'd say, from everything I know, there's a likely chance of that. He certainly has seemed to take to Jemma."

"Jemma adores him. Which of course make me so happy."

Jemma's name coming up reminded Blu of her mother again, and she felt her heart beating faster just thinking about it.

"So how are you feeling about seeing your mother? Maybe this will be a really good thing too," Victoria said.

"Maybe," Blu said. "I'm trying not to get too ahead of myself. It's actually really starting to freak me out."

"How long is she in town for?"

"I'm not sure exactly. She said just a few days, so I suspect not many more after our coffee meeting," Blu said.

"So you would still have time to take Jemma to see her probably."

Victoria said it as if it were a fact, not a question, and

Blu felt her stress level rising just thinking of it.

"I really don't think that's gonna happen," Blu said. "I'm certainly not mentioning anything to Jemma yet, if ever."

The two enjoyed the rest of their coffee, Victoria filling Blu in on their trip to Mexico and Blu suddenly wishing she could escape to Mexico before her meeting the next day.

Victoria laughed at her friend. "You're going to be just fine. Seriously. You're one of the most resilient—and amazing—women I know. I have the feeling that this is just one more thing that is really going to work out for you."

Blu loved this about her friend. She was one of the most positive and supportive people she knew. She got up from the table to give Victoria a hug.

"Thank you so much. For everything, I mean. For being such a great listener, for sure."

"As have you—been a good friend to me as well." Victoria grinned. "And on that note, I think you should let me do you a favor tonight."

"What's that?" Blu asked.

"Let Jemma sleep over and you and Chase can have what sounds like a much needed night alone."

"Really?" Blu grinned.

The girls would be starting back to school again on Monday, and they hadn't seen each other in over a week, so it seemed like a good plan.

Blu hugged Victoria again before calling to Jemma to come down and say goodbye; the girl happily agreed to the sleepover plans, convincing Blu that she didn't need anything from home. Claire would loan her pjs and anything else that she needed.

Blu pulled her phone out from her purse to text Chase as she walked the short distance back to her place.

J is spending the night at Claire's. Do u wanna have our own sleepover tonight??? xo

She smiled after sending it, delighted about the way she was feeling about their relationship. And this even amidst all my stress, she thought. She heard her phone ding with an incoming text.

Yes!! I'll bring the champagne AND cook us a sexy dinner. Be ready. ;)

And another ding, right after.

Love u!

She laughed, texting back the words that she hadn't thought would be coming out of her mouth anytime soon with Chase—or with anyone for that matter. She did love him. God, she loved him a lot. And it wasn't quite so scary any more

The walls were coming down. She could feel it. Her thoughts turned towards the meeting tomorrow. She only hoped that when it came to her mother, she'd left enough to protect herself—to protect Jemma. She couldn't relax that much. There was a reason she'd learned to be so hard and so protective of her daughter. Now was not the time to loosen up on those things. She was sure about that.

CHAPTER 17

Blu woke up to the delicious smell of bacon, grinning as she was reminded of Chase and the wonderful night that they'd spent together. She felt completely content and loved in a way that she'd never felt before. She pulled the covers up around her face, wanting to spend just a few more moments in bed with her thoughts, eager as she was to kiss the man downstairs cooking for her.

She glanced over at the clock beside her bed, noting the time. In two hours she'd be driving to meet her mother. God, the thought made her heart pound. Even now, she debated canceling, but every time she thought of doing so, she reminded herself of the possibility of her mom's turning up at the house, and that was the last thing that she'd want. For Jemma to see her.

She sighed. No, she was doing the right thing. She was sure of it now. She was very curious to see her mother after the brief phone conversation they'd had. She had sounded so different. She'd find out soon enough, Blu thought as she finally got out of bed, pulling on her thick terry robe and making her way downstairs towards her gorgeous man as well as the food that she'd guessed was waiting for her in the kitchen.

She stopped in the doorway to the kitchen, unnoticed by Chase, who was reading the newspaper and sipping his coffee at the breakfast table. The fact that he was shirtless shocked her in a good way, causing her to smile at her unbelievable luck to have found a man who was not only one of the kindest people she'd ever met, but sexy as hell too.

Chase glanced over at her just then, his face erupting in a big grin as he got up to walk towards her. As if he was reading her mind, his hands came around her small waist and his lips crushed hers in a way that made Blu consider leading him back up to the bedroom. God, she loved how passionate he was. It was hard to resist. She laughed at all of the thoughts going on in her head.

Chase pulled away to look at her. "Hey, what's so funny?" He smiled.

"Oh, if you could read my mind right now," Blu said, teasing him.

"Oh yeah? What's in that beautiful, sexy mind of yours?" he teased her back.

"Everything that I don't have time for this morning." She grinned, taking his hand as she made her way into the kitchen. "Something smells fantastic, by the way."

Chase led her over to the small table. The cool morning breeze coming in from the ocean felt lovely, and the fact that this amazing man was serving her breakfast made the morning feel like something out of a movie.

"You sit. Let me get you a cup of coffee," Chase said.

Blu accepted the coffee that he handed her, knowing that he'd made her favorite Italian blend, strong and black, just the way she liked her first cup.

Chase proceeded to lay out a beautiful spread of omelets, bacon, and fruit for the both of them, and suddenly Blu was famished as she dug into it all.

"Oh my god. This is so good," Blu said, barely swallowing the food in her mouth before speaking.

"Do you like it?" Chase grinned as he too dug into his own food. "I figured that you'd have a long day ahead of you, and I know that you usually don't take time for more than toast and coffee in the mornings."

"That is correct," Blu said between mouthfuls. "And I do appreciate it—and you—very much."

Chase reached across the table for her hand. "And I appreciate you very much—especially after last night." He winked.

Blu felt her face growing slightly warm, feeling embarrassed, but also more comfortable with him than she'd ever felt. "Well, I should say the same—oh magnificent lover of mine," she teased.

"I like the sound of that—being your lover." He laughed, then put on a more serious face. "But you do know that I want more than that? To be clear."

"Well, to be clear—I want more than that too," Blu grinned, really enjoying their playful morning banter.

What would it be like to have this every day with him?

She tried to put the thought out of her head for the time being. There'd be time for making plans about their relationship later. Her stomach lurched as her thoughts turned to the upcoming meeting with her mother. She hoped she'd be able to make plans anyways.

Chase looked thoughtful; Blu noticed him watching her as she finished her breakfast, enjoying the easy silence and the beautiful view out the nearby window.

"So how are you feeling?" Chase asked. "About your meeting, I mean?"

Blu took a deep breath as she considered the question. She'd had such a mix of emotions, none of which were exactly pleasant. "I'm not sure. I do feel nervous and also very skeptical. Part of me wonders still if I should just cancel, go with my first instinct to not see her at all. I mean, I could do that."

"Right. You could," Chase agreed, but Blu knew there was more on his mind.

"But?" Blu said.

"But wouldn't you always wonder about it? About her and everything that she's said about being clean now? About how much she's changed?"

"Yes, there's that, and also the fact that I'm guessing she knows where I live because of the website. Truthfully, that more than my curiosity is probably what's driving me not to cancel. The fact that I don't wanna risk her coming here—and Jemma seeing her." Even the thought of that now made her feel ill.

Chase was nodding his head.

"But yeah, I suppose that I am curious too." Blu paused for a moment, gathering her thoughts. "She really did sound so different on the phone."

"Well, I'm proud of you." He squeezed her hand. "For taking the chance. I know it's not an easy thing for you at all."

Blu nodded, grateful once again for Chase's steady presence these past few weeks.

"I'm here for you, and I know that Gigi, Douglas, and Lia are here for you as well. If something goes wrong, you'll have the help that you need to make it okay." He was looking intently at her from across the table. "I promise you that, Blu. That everything's going to be okay."

And she believed him.

Blu sat waiting in the coffee shop, sipping her latte and trying to calm her nerves. She'd suggested a popular spot that she knew would be easy to find, and was happy that she'd arrived fifteen minutes early to choose a table and try to relax a little bit after her racing thoughts during the drive down. She chose a table in the corner where she had a good vantage point for seeing the people as they walked into the cafe.

Her mind flashed to the last time that she'd actually seen her mother. Blu had mistakenly given her the address of her apartment one time and she'd turned up, pounding on her door and begging for help. Not wanting to disturb the neighbors, Blu had let her inside, disturbed by her black eye but not surprised at all. Nothing had surprised her about her mother at that time—she'd seen it all. The bruises, the track marks on her arm, the dirty hair, and the stench of someone who couldn't be bothered to bathe.

That wasn't the first time that she'd asked for Blu's help either. She always needed money, needed something that Blu had discovered that she couldn't give her. She'd tried; she'd tried a lot when she was younger. She wanted to believe that she could be strong enough for her mother. That once she had moved out—away from Harold—her mother would somehow find the courage to get some help too. But that never happened.

Things had only gone from bad to worse. Jemma was born and then Blu's mother was headed off to prison for at least a year, she'd been told. No chance of the baby getting to know her, and Blu knew that it was for the best. She wasn't an influence that Blu had ever wanted the child to grow up around. That had been nine years ago, yet it was really hard for Blu to imagine her mother walking through that door as anyone other than that sad woman from her past.

Blu glanced at her phone to check the time and when she looked back towards the door, she saw her. Her heart beat quickly and she had to take a few deep breaths as she searched her brain for a cue as to how to react to this woman walking towards her with a big smile on her face. A woman who looked nothing like the one that Blu had been imagining.

CHAPTER 18

This woman, walking towards her in the cafe, held a vague resemblance to the one of Blu's earliest childhood memories. The good memories, before everything went bad. Before Blu started school and before her mom met Harold; she had distant memories of a happy home back then. One that had the normal everyday stresses of that of a single woman trying to raise a young daughter on her own, but she remembered the laughter during that time, when it was just her and her mom. And the woman standing beside her now looked like an older version of that younger, happier mom.

"Blu?" She was awkwardly standing next to her at the small table and Blu knew that she was waiting for her to stand up, to allow her the hug she'd been waiting these past days to administer. But she just couldn't bring herself to do it. There's was nothing comfortable about the moment, and all she could do was gesture towards the seat across from her.

"Have—have a seat. Please. Let's get you something to drink." Blu didn't recognize her own strained voice. She called the waitress over, and her mom ordered a black coffee. With the drink ordered, the two were left staring at one another across the table. Her mother seemed much more at ease than Blu did, and this oddly made her more curious about how this was going to go.

She was staring at Blu with a wide smile. "You look so great. Incredible, really."

"Thank you," Blu managed to croak out.

"Thank you again, so much, for meeting me. I know this must seem pretty sudden to you."

Blu nodded her head as her mom continued, trying not to be too distracted by the way she looked to miss what she was saying. But she had to admit that Linda looked very healthy, not at all like someone who was doing drugs, living the lifestyle that had haunted Blu's memories whenever she'd let herself remember her mother and earlier times.

"Sorry, what was that?" She was very distracted, and needed to get a grip so that she could pay attention to what her mother was saying.

Her mother smiled. "I was just saying how amazing it was to see you on TV. You always did have an incredible sense of fashion. Even as a little girl, playing dress-up."

Blu pasted a fake smile on her face and nodded. In her head, she recalled that her memories of playing dress-up had to do with escaping the nightmare that was playing out in her living room. Usually one to do with her mom getting punched around by Harold or both of them passed out in a drunken stupor.

"How—how long are you in town?" Blu couldn't think of what to say, and her own feelings of awkwardness didn't seem to be getting any easier.

"I'm leaving on Saturday."

Blu counted four more days in her head.

"Have you been here before—to San Diego?" The small talk was nearly unbearable, but she didn't know her way around it. It was just all too weird.

"No. I—I only came here to see you." She looked at Blu tentatively, as if waiting for her approval to continue.

Blu looked up, granting her the go-ahead with her eye contact, which wasn't easy for her. She knew it was necessary if anything real was going to come of this meeting. And she'd come this far.

"I had to see you—to tell you that I've changed." She reached across the table for her daughter's hand and Blu instinctively pulled it away.

"You do look good," Blu said quietly. "I wouldn't have recognized you. Anywhere else, I mean."

"It's been a long time, Blu. A lot's happened. I'm not the person that you last saw all those years ago. Before you—before you and Jessica left."

Her mom had been in prison when she left and Blu had never looked back. For all these years since, she really hadn't known if her mom was alive or dead. Either case was plausible, and each was one that Blu had been willing to live with when she left.

After several minutes of silence, Blu spoke, quietly

again. "How long?"

Her mom looked at her with a question in her eyes.

"How long have you been sober?" Blu held her breath without realizing it. She knew what the road to recovery was like for addicts. She had witnessed a few different periods during her teenage years when her mom had attended rehab, coming out a "new person", ready to take on the world. Only to have everything come crashing down again, usually within a few months, always having to do with Harold being let back into the house. She knew the pattern. She'd decided after the fourth time that rehab wouldn't work for her mom. That was the day she'd given up all hope for her.

"Being in prison changed me. I was there for one year and let out on good behavior. I'd been clean the whole time, which was a record for me. I did mess up several times after that, but I've been sober now for four years."

Blu was shocked, and she was sure that it showed on her face as she tried to find her words. "You've been sober for four years?"

"Four years, two months, and three days." Her mother didn't miss a beat. "I still go to meetings, working my plan. Every day. Day by day."

Blu was genuinely at a loss for words. For four years her mom had been sober. It was something she'd not expected in all the various scenarios that had played out in her mind since she'd received that first email from her.

"And Harold?" She had to ask. She knew that this

was the only other question that mattered.

"Harold and I are done. We were done long ago when I realized that I was never going to be able to stay sober if we were together."

Blu was nodding her head, a little seed of hope beginning to make itself known to her.

"I'm not going to lie. It wasn't easy to disengage myself from him. Well, he didn't make it easy. Even now, I still get the odd phone call from him, begging me to see him." She looked Blu in the eye. "But I don't want him any more. I don't want anything to do with that life."

Blu looked at this woman sitting in front of her, with a face worn by rough times and the signs of past neglect, but she was clear-eyed and beautiful to Blu. And God, suddenly Blu desperately wanted to believe her.

Just as fast as the thought entered her mind, she hit against her remaining wall of doubt, up and yet to be knocked down. She still had to be careful. She had Jemma to think about—to protect.

Her mom looked relaxed sitting across from her, not anxious as she waited for Blu to say something in response to what she'd just told her about Harold.

"That's really great. Really great." She didn't know what to say.

"Thank you," her mom said quietly, and Blu thought it looked like she wanted to say more.

"What is it?"

"I just want to be totally honest with you."

Blu felt herself tense up a bit as she waited for her mom to continue.

"It's nothing bad, really. Just that because of the mistakes I've made in the past, I'm still working on stuff—other stuff too I mean."

Blu didn't know if she should ask more questions or just leave it alone. Finally she spoke. "Are you okay?" *And what will I offer her if she says that she isn't?*

"Yes, I'm fine. Really." She smiled and Blu believed her.

CHAPTER 19

Blu found herself little by little believing everything that her mom was telling her, which was pretty incredible to her. Letting her guard down with Chase lately really did seem to have her looking at life through a different lens. She seemed to be turning into someone who had the ability to trust, which was a novel idea for a skeptic such as herself. She wanted to trust her mom. Sitting here across from her now, she wanted this more than anything.

"Blu?"

"Yes?"

"Will—will you tell me about Jessica?"

Blu could tell by the way she'd spoken that it was a difficult thing for her to ask for, and she didn't blame her for feeling that way. But if she did really trust her gut about all this, her mom deserved to know some things, didn't she?

Blu took a deep breath. "Yes." She smiled at her mom, who was eagerly leaning forward as Blu picked up her phone to find a picture to show her.

"Here she is." She showed her a picture taken just last week of Jemma on the beach, her long blonde hair blowing in the breeze, her grin as wide as ever.

Her mom smiled. "She's so lovely. Isn't she?" She glanced down at the picture again and Blu noticed tears making their way down her cheeks.

"Her name is Jemma." Blu said quietly. "I changed both of our names when—when we left New York.

Her mom looked up. "Yes, I assumed that you did."

Blu nodded, knowing that it wasn't a secret by this point.

"I did try to find you. Not right away when I got out of prison. I was still too caught up in trying to make something work. But after I'd been sober—for about a year—a friend of mine who's good with the Internet tried to help me. We searched all kinds of records, but nothing was turning up."

Blu nodded, knowing that she would have been hard to find—that she'd made it that way on purpose when she moved across the country to start a new life for her and Jemma. Now it made her kind of sad, thinking about her mom doing so much better and searching, trying to find them. But she'd made the choices that were best for them, determined to not have any regrets when it came to Jemma and what was ultimately best for her.

"Then after all this time, to look up and see you on the TV—it was like a miracle, honestly." She smiled and wiped the tears away from her cheeks with a swipe of her hand. "I was so proud of—I am so proud of you."

Blu smiled. It did feel good to hear her mom say that to her. To share even a bit of the amazement at the success that she'd had as a designer with her mom was something that she'd never thought would happen. To her, that was the miracle. That the two of them were sitting together now.

"What you've done for yourself—despite my pathetic or nonexistent attempts at raising you—is incredible, Blu. I hope that you know that."

Blu grew serious. There were many things that her mother didn't know about her—didn't have a clue about the kind of life that she and Jemma had had.

"It hasn't always been easy—or good," Blu said. "And I've—I've worked hard. Really hard," she said, watching her mother's face as she spoke. She saw a recognition in her eyes. In many ways, the two women were nothing alike, but in some ways Blu considered that they might be very similar, after finding out more about her mother and the last four years of her life. They'd both struggled, for sure, and if Blu had to guess, she thought her mom was still working through some of that struggle now.

Blu continued. "And I've also been lucky." She flashed to Arianna and everything that she'd learned and been given by her best friend. "Lucky in that I've had some incredible friends to help me along the way. Jemma has been a part of that too. It wasn't always easy for us these past years, but we've had people that loved us—that had become a family of sorts to us."

Blu didn't say this to hurt her mother, even though she recognized that the words had the potential to cut deeply. She only wanted to open up just a bit, the same way that her mother had with her. If she was going to be real with her, the good came with the bad, and some parts of it were not going to be easy for her mother to know or want to relive. But she seemed open. She was taking in Blu's words, without interruption.

After a few moments of oddly comfortable silence, her mother spoke again.

"I'm glad to hear that you and Jemma have found such love and happiness. I never wanted less for either of you. I hope that you know that."

Blu nodded.

"Even back when I was strung out and going to prison, I understood why you did what you did. Why you left with Jemma." She wiped away the quick tears again. "You were brave and determined even back then. I remember thinking that, when Harold showed up and told me that you were gone. I never blamed you for leaving even back then. Even when I became sober. You knew, better than I, what was for the best. You always knew that, even as a little girl."

This time it was Blu's turn to wipe away tears. Everything her mother was telling her was like a salve to an open wound, applied little by little, bringing just a hint of relief. She could feel her heart opening up to her. What was a glimmer of hope now seemed a real possibility as the two spoke honestly to one another. Woman to woman. Mother to daughter. It appeared to Blu to be with no agenda, just a desire for honest communication.

"Thank you for telling me that," Blu said, trying to regain her composure. "If I'm being honest, it has haunted me over the years. Not so much the decisions that I made back then, but the fact that I had completely cut all ties with you. I had to, but it didn't stop me from wondering, from hoping that you were okay—that you were alive."

Her mother reached across the table for her hand, and this time Blu didn't pull away. They had said so much during their short conversation, and yet Blu knew that there was so much more to say.

Blu looked at the time on her phone, knowing that it was getting to be time to leave but not quite ready to end the conversation with her mother.

"Would you want to get together again tomorrow? Maybe we could go for a short walk on the beach or something?" Blu had blurted out the invitation before taking any time to second-guess herself.

Her mother smiled in a way that lit up her whole face. "Yes, I'd like that a lot. Would—would it be possible to bring Jemma?"

Blu froze, her heart beating fast. No, she wasn't ready for that yet. There was too much to be said yet, too much to explain to Jemma.

"No. I'm sorry. But I just don't think I can do that." She saw the disappointment in her mom's face. "I'm not—I'm not saying never. It just seems too soon."

"It's okay. Really." Her mother smiled.

Blu guessed it was in an attempt to reassure her and get back on track that everything really was going to be okay.

"I'd love to go for a walk with you. I'll take any time that I can get before I have to leave."

"Great, then we'll plan for a walk tomorrow morning. Say for about ten o'clock?"

Her mom nodded her head in agreement.

"Why don't I drop you back at your hotel so then I'll know where to pick you up tomorrow? Are you staying close by?" Blu asked her mom.

She thought her mom looked slightly embarrassed when she mentioned the motel chain where she was staying.

"It's no problem. I think that's right on my way home, actually," Blu said.

CHAPTER 20

Blu dropped her mom off at her motel, noting that it wasn't exactly in the best part of town. She had a moment of thinking that it would be so easy to have her mom pack up her things and move her to a nicer place—a hotel where she'd be safe and lavished with some comforts—but then stopped herself. This was something that she had to be careful of, and dropping her off had put in front of Blu what had been a doubt in the back of her mind.

Her mom hadn't mentioned money at all, but from the looks of where she was staying, Blu guessed that a lot hadn't changed with her mother's financial situation. She'd grown up poor, and it was a life that Blu was very familiar with.

Blu had seen it all, really, when it came to finances; she'd worked her butt off to provide a meager lifestyle for herself and Jemma once she'd moved to the west coast, so that Jemma could have more than what she'd had growing up. And eventually came the life they had now, the lifestyle that Arianna had made possible for them.

She pushed the doubts aside as she continued the drive home. The solution would be to not offer her mom any money. She'd know soon enough if money was her motive for coming here, and so far she'd given Blu no indication that it had anything to do with her wanting to see her.

Blu saw her mother two more times over the next two days. They went for walks on the beach followed by coffee and long lunches. They talked a lot, and many things that needed to be said were said, but there were still many layers to peel back—at least where Blu was concerned. She hadn't yet fully let her guard down—fully letting her mom into her life—but surprisingly she was more open to the idea than she'd ever been. She didn't know if she'd ever be able to fully trust her; but little by little, she could see that her mom seemed genuine, that she definitely was not on drugs—Blu felt that she would have detected that right away, had she been lying about it.

After her third meeting with her mother Blu was driving home just in time to pick Jemma up from school. She'd been playing phone tag, as usual, with Lia, so when she saw her ringing in on her phone, she pulled off the highway to take the call.

"Lia?"

"Blu, hi. So sorry it's been so difficult to connect." Lia's voice over the phone, so happy and carefree-sounding, made Blu instantly feel relaxed about speaking with her about her mother.

She didn't have a clear idea of what Lia's advice would be but she believed her to be objective, even though she'd been such a proponent of Blu's seeing her mother in the first place.

"Oh, no worries at all. I know that you are busy—that you have a life other than doling out your great advice to me." Blu laughed and Lia did too on the other end of the line.

"Are you kidding? Seriously, I always have time for you."

Blu believed her and the thought made her smile.

"Tell me everything. I'm so anxious to hear how it's been going with your mother," Lia said.

"Yeah, that's what I wanted to talk to you about." Blu could hardly contain the excitement she was feeling now that she was finally talking to her friend about it, and the idea of that both astounded and terrified her. She'd come so far in terms of her feelings about her mother.

"Go on. Tell me then." Lia was laughing on the other end. "Have you seen her more than once? What's she like?"

Blu told her about their first meeting—how it was uncomfortable at first, but how amazed she was at how good her mother looked and how clear-headed she'd been, something that Blu really hadn't been expecting if she was being honest.

Lia listened attentively, waiting for Blu to finish telling her all about their first meeting in the coffee shop.

"And I've seen her every day since then," Blu went on breathlessly. "She's leaving on Saturday, and things have been going so well that I thought we should really take advantage of the time that we have here now together."

"That makes sense," Lia was saying on the other end of the line. "Blu, I'm so glad that it's been going well. You're glad, then, that you decided to see her, I take it?" Blu could imagine her wide smile across the miles.

"Yes, I'm so glad."

"And Jemma?" She detected the timidity of her friend's question. "Has she seen Jemma?"

"No." Blu took a deep breath. "That's part of what I wanted to talk to you about, actually."

"Okay," Lia said.

"She did ask me that first day if she could see her—when we were making plans for the next day. And it—it caught me totally by surprise. I wasn't ready then at all. And I told her that, which she did understand. We'd barely spent any time together at that point—well, not that we've had tons of time since then, but our talks have gotten more in-depth, and I can't help but start to feel so much more at ease with her."

"So, now you're thinking about it—about introducing her to Jemma?" Lia asked.

"Yes. Well, she hasn't asked again and I don't think she would, given my first response to her. She seems happy that the two of us are spending time together before she leaves. And, I dunno. I guess it's just something I've been thinking about as the time gets closer to her leaving."

"That makes sense," Lia said evenly. "Do you think Jemma would want to meet her?"

"Yes. That's not even a question in my mind. As you know, she's been asking a lot of questions lately about who her grandma is, mostly because of all the time that she's been spending with Claire—who is quite close to her own grandmother, I suspect. It seems like something maybe I should do for her—for both of them." She felt more confused now though, as she was talking about it out loud. She sighed. "Oh, I dunno. Maybe it's better left alone. Who knows what could happen? I could be wrong about my mother."

"Yes, you could be." Lia paused. "But what does your heart tell you? Your instinct?"

Lia knew her well and she knew how much Blu had changed over the past months.

Letting her walls down with Chase had really changed her as a person, softened her a bit. Her friends all noticed it, commented on it. There was a time when Blu would have laughed outright at Lia's question about letting her heart lead her. She came from a past that did not trust one's heart—a past where she learned that she had to protect herself at any price. And a big part of that had been shutting her heart off to anything as deceiving as her own emotions.

But she thought long and hard about Lia's question to her now. It was valid. She knew that. "Hmm. That's a good question. Right now in the moment, after having just had a great long lunch with her, I'd say that I can't think of a reason not to let her see Jemma. But ask me later tonight and I'll probably have a different answer." She laughed, but the conversation really wasn't funny to her. It was driving her a bit mad actually—trying to make this decision—and she was still waiting for Lia to tell her what to do—even thought she knew that Lia would only help her to make the best decision for herself.

"Well, how 'bout asking yourself what the worst thing that could happen would be?"

Blu didn't have to think twice about that one, but it was something that oddly she knew that she trusted her mom about. Therefore, the worst thing she could imagine happening really wasn't so bad, considering how happy it could make both Jemma and her mother to finally meet.

"Okay. That helps, I guess."

"Maybe sleep on it? See how you feel in the morning?" Lia said.

"Yeah, I think I'm gonna have to; but tomorrow is really my last chance before she leaves," Blu said.

"Don't feel pressured. It might be the last time right now, but the important thing is that the two of you are in contact now."

Blu was nodding her head as Lia continued.

"You can always decide one thing now and a different thing later, right? I mean you and Jemma can go there in the future—when you're feeling more comfortable."

"That is a very good point, one worth making."

Blu felt a great sense of relief all of a sudden. Lia was right. She'd didn't have to feel pressured. She could trust herself to make the right decision—for Jemma. She just needed to remain focused on what she felt was the best thing for her daughter, and she would be fine. They'd all be fine.

"Thank you so much, Lia."

"Really? I hardly feel that I was very helpful, even though I desperately want to be." Lia laughed, and Blu felt the pang of missing her friend even thought they'd just seen each other.

"Yes, really. You always make me feel calm about things." Blu smiled.

"Good. I'm glad," Lia said.

"And on that note, I should go before I'm running late to pick up Jemma at school, which will leave me feeling anything but calm." The two women laughed as they said goodbye and hung up, vowing to speak in the next few days about the outcome of Blu's decision.

CHAPTER 21

Blu sat cuddled up with Chase in front of the fireplace. Jemma had gone to bed, and the evening temperature coming in through the windows was the perfect invitation for a nice fire and a bottle of wine. It was one of the things Blu most appreciated about her home, second only to the stunning views of the ocean from nearly every window of the house.

Since she and Chase had grown closer, these romantic nights by the fire had become a welcome refuge after a day of working nonstop on her clothing, or lately, dealing with the thoughts that stressed her out about how she was handling things in regards to her mother.

Tonight was one of those nights when she was looking forward to Chase helping her to sort out her feelings about her mother. He'd become her constant sounding board, her best friend. She looked at him now, a huge grin on her face.

"What's up with that grin?" Chase teased her, not giving her a chance to reply before he covered her mouth with an intense kiss. It left her pressing up against him as she tried to tell him with her body what was making her so blissfully happy.

She pulled away a bit to look him in the eye. "You make me insane with happiness," she said finally as he replied to her words with another kiss, more passionate than the last.

"And you—you just make me crazy—for wanting you." He laughed and handed her the glass of wine from the coffee table in front of them. "Tell me how the day was. You saw your mother again this morning, right?"

Blu nodded, taking a sip of her wine. "Yes, we went for another long walk on the beach and then went for a great lunch at this cute little place near there."

"That's good." He kissed her on the top of her head as she nestled her cheek against his chest. "Do you feel like you've gotten a better sense of her? In terms of what she's doing here, how you're feeling in general about your relationship—all that stuff that you were concerned about."

Blu tilted her head back, trying to look stern, yet failing as she was smiling again a few seconds later.

"—And rightly so, I mean." Chase backtracked on his last statement, kissing her on the tip of her nose. "Seriously, you have all the reason in the world not to trust her. No one would blame you for that, least of all me. I know it was a huge step for you to take to even consider letting her in your life, so I'm incredibly proud of you for that."

Blu turned slightly as she lay next to him, putting her

arms around his waist, hugging him close to her. "Thank you for that. It means a lot to me. And yes, I agree. I have come a very long ways—and not just in terms of my mother. I've not always been this much of a sucker for a good-looking chef, ya know." It was her turn to tease him, and he laughed in response.

"So, back to more serious topics—which I'll not let you distract me from."

"Yes, I know. I do need to talk to you, actually."

"Okay," Chase replied. "Go on. I'll do my best."

"So, tomorrow is the last day that I'm seeing my mother before she leaves. We'll be walking in the morning and—well, I've hardly made any decisions about this, but I'm toying with the idea of taking Jemma to see her after school."

"Oh yeah?" Chase said, and she thought he sounded surprised.

Well, she had been adamantly opposed to it ever since the first meeting when her mother had asked. But since then—well, things had changed and she was trying to change—to be more open these days. It had been a huge step for her to even see her mother. Allowing her to see Jemma was a great big "heart on her sleeve" deal—it was the one thing that her mother could really hurt that heart with—if she wanted to. But even as the thought entered Blu's mind, she knew that she didn't have to worry about that.

"Huh?" Blu said, realizing that Chase had been asking

her a question.

"I was just asking how that idea was making you feel."

"I'm kinda all over the place, if I'm being honest. One minute it absolutely feels like the right thing to do, the next minute the idea terrifies me and I think that I must be a little bit crazy to even consider it." She laughed, trying to lighten her own mood—which was starting to feel a little stressed out.

"Do you have to decide now?"

"Well, tomorrow is her last day here before she leaves, so I do have to decide soon, don't I?" She remembered how she felt after Lia's suggestion, though, and filled Chase in on the conversation.

"So, wait and see how you feel after the morning," he said.

"And should I mention anything to her?"

"I wouldn't. Unless you're sure, I mean. It seems a bit cruel to get her hopes up unless you're one hundred percent sure that its gonna happen." He reached down for her hands, intertwining his fingers with her own. "You'll know what the right thing to do is. And if it's not tomorrow, it doesn't mean that you are shutting the door on the idea forever. Try to take the pressure off of yourself."

Blu was quiet for a minute. "Wise words, my handsome lover."

They both laughed instantaneously. "Your lover, huh? Shall we sneak up to the bedroom so that I can practice up on that description of me?"

Blu laughed and was on her feet pulling him up within seconds, all thoughts about her mother, and what she would do the next day, temporarily leaving her mind.

CHAPTER 22

Blu was early to pick up Jemma for once. She was happy for the quiet time to sit by herself and reflect on the time that she'd spent with her mother that morning. They'd gone for a walk at the beach, which had become a nice little routine for them over the past few days. She was sorry that it was ending, if she was being honest with herself. Saying goodbye had been bittersweet but in the end, she'd decided that she just didn't feel comfortable with her earlier thoughts about taking Jemma to see Linda. She had to trust her instinct when it came to Jemma—she always had, and now was not the time to stop.

So they'd enjoyed their morning walk and lunch after. And at the end of it there were hugs and promises to phone soon and keep in touch. She didn't have any real doubts that her mother wouldn't keep in touch, and she was fully prepared to take it one step at a time, getting to know one another, and then eventually one day Jemma and Blu's mother would meet. Blu tried to ignore the feeling in the pit of her stomach thinking about that as the kids started filing out of the school for pick-up.

"Can we go for some ice cream?" Jemma said, tossing her backpack into the backseat of the car.

"Excuse me, little Ms. Manners—how about 'Hello, Mom. How was your day?'" Blu shook her head, smiling but thinking that Jemma's attitude really had been suffering lately.

"Sorry, Mom." She leaned over to give her mom a quick kiss and flash her a big smile, and all was forgiven by Blu. "So, how was your day then?" Jemma grinned, teasing now.

"My day was great, thanks for asking." Blu hadn't told Jemma anything about her grandma being in town and fully intended to keep that information to herself. "How was school?"

"Oh you know. Good, TGIF, all that jazz."

Blu laughed at her silly tone. "Well, what do you think about seeing if Claire can spend the night tomorrow and I'll take you two to a movie or something?" she said as she pulled out of the school parking lot.

"She can't," Jemma replied. "Her grandma is coming to town for the weekend." She looked at Blu before continuing on. "I'm sure that they'll be baking delicious cookies or something all weekend." She was fake pouting now, but the simple statement hit Blu hard.

"Okay—well, I'm sure that I could bake some—"

"—Mom!" Jemma interrupted. "When are you gonna tell me about my grandma? About my family. I'm not a child any more, you know. You haven't told me one single thing about any of them—my grandma or even my dad."

Blu's mind was racing. Was it a coincidence that Jemma was bringing this up now, or did she need to listen to her gut telling her that it was wrong for her to keep her mother and Jemma apart when the child so desperately wanted it—when she could give her some of those answers—at least the answers that she thought would satisfy many of the questions that Jemma had been having lately.

She pulled the car off the busy side street she'd been driving on.

"Mom, what you are doing?"

"I—I need to talk to you—to tell you something," she said, looking Jemma in the eyes.

"Okay," Jemma said in exasperation. "What is it? Why are you looking so serious all of the sudden?"

Blu took a deep breath. "Your grandma is in town."

Jemma's eyes grew wide. "She is? Where does she live?"

"She lives in New York—where I grew up. You know, I've talked to you about living upstate before."

"Yeah, you mean, whenever you're trying to remind me of how good I have it," Jemma teased, then seemed to remember the bigger topic at hand. "But so what do you mean that she's here? Where? Mom, can I see her?"

She was obviously excited, and there was no turning back now. "Well, that's what I was thinking about—but there are some things that I have to tell you. Things that you are just going to have to trust me about. Deal?"

"Okay, deal," Jemma said quickly, and it was the sort of spur-of-the-moment agreement that Blu could never count on with the child.

"So, you've not really heard anything about your grandma—my mother—because she and I haven't gotten along for a very long time. In fact, it was only this week that I've spoken with her since I was much younger."

Jemma was nodding her head, listening intently.

"So, she has wanted to meet you but I wasn't sure." Blu met Jemma's eyes carefully.

"Why? Why wouldn't you want her to see me?"

Blu didn't blame Jemma for the confusion. She was finding it very hard now to explain anything that would make sense, even to a child. "It's not that I didn't want her to meet you—to spend time with you—because I know that could be really good. I just didn't—don't want you to get your hopes up about having her in your life—" She met Jemma's eyes again with her own. "—if I thought she was going to have any problems following through, I mean."

Jemma was quiet for a moment, and Blu wondered how confused she had just made the poor girl.

"Well, I'm pretty sure if there are any problems, you're gonna help me with them," Jemma said so matter-of-factly that Blu laughed.

"That is a very good point. And I think I could do

that." She smiled at her daughter. "What do you think then? Shall we go see her? Or try to, anyways, because I'm not even sure that she'll be at the motel."

Jemma was nodding her head, grinning widely. "Yes, let's surprise her. Do you think she will be surprised to see me?"

"Oh, yes. I think she will be very surprised."

Blu felt a strange sense of calm as she headed towards the motel. She could try to call her first—it would be the polite thing to do—but she also could imagine the big smile on Linda's face when Blu suddenly turned up with Jemma beside her. She wanted to give her mom that gift. It absolutely felt like the right thing to do, and now she was very excited at how the day was turning out—for both of them—Jemma and her mother.

Jemma was all smiles as Blu made the drive, chatting away about the things she wanted to tell her grandmother about school, Claire, and any number of miscellaneous bits of information that she thought she should know about her. As they got very close, Jemma suddenly pointed by the side of the street.

"Hey, Mom. We went by here on the bus the other day."

Blu glanced over at her, for a minute confused about what she was talking about. "What, honey? What bus?"

"With Claire and her sister—the other day when we took the bus—remember, I told you about it?"

Blu nodded her head. "The bus came all the way

down here, honey? Are you sure?"

"Yes, I'm sure. I remember that little shop on the corner there."

Blu was nodding but had become distracted, as they were pulling into the motel parking lot. What the hell? She couldn't believe her eyes as she pulled discreetly into a parking space that allowed her to see the door of her mother's room facing the parking lot.

Jemma was chatting away, ready to pounce out of the car. "What number is it? Wait—is that her?" She was pointing at Blu's mother, who was standing in the doorway, obviously livid with anger as she yelled at the man standing in front of her.

"Shh. Jemma. Get down, please. We're going to stay in the car right now." Blu had to be sure as she watched the couple arguing. Unbelievably, she'd been right when she first pulled in, thinking that the man she saw with her mother was Harold. Her stomach lurched as she saw him now. Both he and her mother were too caught up in what looked like a very heated argument to pay any attention to Blu and Jemma in the parking lot.

Had he been here all along? The thought occurred to her as she continued to watch them from inside the car. God, how could I really have been that stupid? Once she realized what and who she was looking at, she felt her blood boil. She was more angry than she'd been—maybe ever. If Jemma hadn't been with her, she would have stormed towards them both right away, but she didn't want to create a scene in front of Jemma. It was all she could do to keep from driving away, but she didn't want to draw attention to them.

"Mom, I'm getting out of the car." Jemma was starting to open the door, and Blu put her arm quickly across her to pull the door shut quietly.

"Jemma, no. We're not going to get out now." Her voice was louder than she'd meant it to be, and Jemma was in tears now.

"You promised. I want to see her." Jemma turned to her with a look of defiance, and Blu felt her head spinning as to how to handle the scene in front of her.

Watching her mother and Harold arguing in front of the motel was like a flashback to more than several scenes that she'd witnessed in the trailer park where she'd grown up. She'd been surrounded by yelling and screaming by the pair of them since she was a little girl. It was exactly what she'd wanted to take Jemma away from. The fact that mother and daughter were here now, practically trapped in her car as witnesses with Jemma crying and shouting at her, was possibly one of the worst things Blu could have imagined happening as a result of her decision to bring Jemma here today.

Jemma was crying, silently watching out the window, and there was nothing Blu could do to stop it. She was mesmerized too, watching her mom's arms waving and Harold approaching closer to her in the doorway, looking big and intimidating. Just as she remembered him. She swallowed down the vomit that suddenly burned in her throat. Her hand was on her phone, very close to calling for help if she saw the scene getting any more violent.

Just like that, Harold had turned around and stormed to his motorcycle; it was parked far enough away from where they sat in the parking lot that Blu didn't worry about him spotting them before he sped away. Her mother watched him go, looking angry, wiping at tears with her hand before turning to go back inside the small room.

CHAPTER 23

Blu was trying to clear her head, comfort Jemma, and figure out what to say to her mother all at once. She wasn't going to leave the motel without letting her mother know that she'd seen her—that she knew everything, that it was over.

Jemma was still crying, looking like she was going to spring out of the car any second. She turned her tear-stained face towards Blu. "Who was that man? Can't I go see my grandma now?"

Blu shook her head. "He's no one—just a very bad guy. And no, Jemma, you can't go over there."

"But why?" She was sobbing. "We're already here. Mom."

"Jemma, you're going to have to just listen to me." Blu's voice was stern—maybe the sternest she'd ever been with her daughter. "I'm going to go talk to her for a few minutes, and I need you to promise me that you're going to stay in the car."

Jemma was shaking her head. "No, I'm coming with

you."

"No!" Blu shouted. "You're not." She opened her door and bent down to look her in the eye. "Do as I say." Jemma looked up at Blu, her eyes big. "Do you hear me?"

"Yes." She turned away from her, putting her face back towards the window in defiance.

When Blu was confident that Jemma wasn't going to follow her, she shut and locked all the car doors behind her, taking a deep breath as she quickly walked across the lawn to the door of her mother's motel room. She rapped strong and loudly on the door, nothing prepared to say, but not worried in the least about finding the words. She was not prepared to hold anything back from her mother now. She was much too angry to be concerned with her feelings or how she was about to speak to her.

When her mother opened the door, looking surprised, Blu walked past her across the small room to get out of the path of Jemma's vision from where she watched from the car.

"Blu. Hi. What—"

"What am I doing here?" Blu shouted, finally able to let out some of the pent-up rage she'd been feeling for the last several minutes in the car with Jemma.

Her mother looked genuinely shocked at her outburst, although she was already looking pretty disheveled from her own argument a few moments earlier.

"Yes, what's the matter? Sit down. Let me get you a

glass of water." She started towards the small refrigerator in the corner of the room but Blu stopped her by reaching out to grab her by the arm.

"Don't bother. I'm not staying long." Her anger slipped out so easily in the words directed towards her mother. "I brought Jemma here to see you—we came to surprise you—"

Her mom's face lit up at the mention of Jemma's name. "Really? Where is she?"

Blu noticed her looking towards the windows trying to steal a peek.

"You're not going to see her."

Her mom looked at her, a big question in her eyes.

"I saw you—we saw you—with him—with Harold." It disgusted her to even say his name.

"Blu, that's—that's not—"

"What? It's not what I think? That you've been lying to me this whole time?" Blu interrupted, enraged.

"No, it's not." Her mother looked her in the eye. "I didn't know he was here—in town. I—"

"I don't believe you." Blu screamed, tears stinging her eyes as she desperately tried to keep them from falling. She wouldn't shed a tear over this woman who'd been lying to her face. "What was it? The money? The two of you cooked up some scheme when you saw that I'd finally made something of myself?" Even to her own ear, Blu's voice didn't sound like her own.

"Blu, please. Please listen to me." Tears were

streaming down her mother's face. "I've had no communication with Harold at all. His turning up was a complete surprise to me and it's—he's not someone I want anything to do with. You have to believe me."

"Mom?" The two women both looked up at Jemma, now standing in the doorway of the motel room. Jemma looked at her grandmother, eyes wide.

"Jemma, I told you to stay in the car!" Blu shouted, trying to pull herself together so that the child wouldn't see the full extent of her fury, but the words came out strangled and harsh as she moved across the room, placing herself in between her mother and Jemma—a human shield against the bad that she'd always protected Jemma from.

Blu physically turned Jemma's body around to face the door, away from her mother, who had tears streaming down her face as she looked on in silence from the bed. Blu gave Jemma a slight push to get her on the other side of the door. "Jemma, go to the car now." The child turned around to look at her mother, defiant and ready to argue. Blu glared at her, intent that she make her obey. "Jemma. I mean it." She had won for now, as Jemma stomped to the car, sobbing and screaming that she hated her mother.

Blu turned around to face her mother, visibly shaken and upset as she stood up to speak to her daughter.

Her mother closed her eyes for a moment and Blu could see her taking a deep breath before she spoke.

"Everything I've told you has been true. I have changed, and my coming here—I only came to see you." She brushed away her tears again as she looked at her daughter, pleading with her eyes for Blu to believe her.

But Blu's walls were fully up again—a mother guarding her child. She was unshaken in her anger. She walked across the room to the still-open door, turning towards her mother before she stepped outside. "I don't believe you. I'll never believe you again."

She could hear her mother sobbing as she walked away without looking back.

CHAPTER 24

Blu stormed around to the driver's seat of the car, glimpsing her mother standing in the doorway of her motel room, begging her to come back. God, how have I been so foolish, to believe any of this has been real? She wiped her angry tears away as she started the car, looking at Jemma sitting next to her.

"Jemma, put your seatbelt on."

Jemma was ignoring her, waving to Blu's mother and crying in loud sobs.

"I wanna see her," she cried. "Why can't I just see her, Mom?"

"Jemma, I said put your seatbelt on." Her words were louder now, as she turned the car around to leave, not at all sure if she was sane enough to be driving. She knew the kind of rage she was feeling wasn't good. She had to try to keep it together.

Jemma finally obeyed, still crying loudly. "Mom, why can't I see her?"

The young girl was as angry as Blu had ever seen her. Blu had to somehow navigate in her brain past all of her own rage, to figure out a way to talk to Jemma that made any sense at all.

"Jemma it's—she's just not good for you to see right now. That man who was there—he's bad news, and I don't want you around her if he's near."

God, what am I doing to her? Some day was Jemma gonna hate her for all the secrets she'd kept from her? Everything had just gone so wrong. Damn her mother for putting her through this. For putting Jemma through this.

"I just wanted to see my grandma," Jemma spoke quietly now, the tears still streaming down her face. "It's not fair that I don't know her at all. I hate you for not letting me see her, Mom, I really do."

The words stung, a dagger straight to Blu's heart as she tried to think what to say to the young girl, how to get through this. What would she herself expect now from Linda? Was she going to make things difficult for her now that Blu was aware of Harold? If she was lying about him, Blu was sure that her mother was lying about everything. Except for the drugs. She was sober. Blu did believe her when it came to that. She'd never have been able to pull off looking and sounding as sober as she'd been, so that was one thing. Then it had to be about the money.

She glanced at Jemma sitting next to her, her hands balled up into fists, tears still streaming down her face. For a moment, Blu doubted everything she'd ever said about keeping the truth from Jemma. Maybe she did deserve to know the truth about her. But she pushed those thoughts away. No, she was too young. Blu would tell her when she was older, when she could understand more of why Blu had done what she'd done. That is, if her mother didn't now go back on her word. Blu felt a new panic rising within her. She'd have to phone Douglas, to be ready for that. Nothing had changed. She would still protect Jemma at all costs, even if it meant leaving their life here.

She pulled into their driveway, and Jemma was out the door before they'd even come to a complete stop, slamming it loudly behind her. After shouting again how much she hated Blu, Jemma stormed upstairs, and Blu broke out in a flood of tears, making her way to her own room to be alone with her thoughts. She'd check on Jemma in a little while when they'd both had a little time to themselves. She'd calm down. She always did. And in the meantime Blu would figure out how to talk to her about everything that had happened.

Blu tried to phone Chase, willing him to pick up but knowing that he was working all day, unlikely to do so. She really needed to talk to him. She needed a voice of reason; she knew that he'd be able to calm her down, maybe Jemma too. Maybe Chase would know the right words to say to Jemma.

She recognized the sounds of books being hurled across Jemma's room down the hall. She'd rarely seen her this angry before but she knew that the best thing was to give her some time. She would calm down eventually, and everything would be okay again between them,

But now there are so many more questions to be answered. In the back of her mind, Blu knew that it probably wasn't likely that Jemma was going to forget about her grandma or what Blu had done, keeping them apart. She knew that the can of worms had only just been opened, and as Jemma got older she was going to demand answers. Answers that Blu would have to be willing to answer, or eventually lose her.

Blu sighed and lay down on her bed to close her eyes for just a minute. If only she could just step back in time, maybe she wouldn't have done Fashion Week at all. Would she have even bothered with her clothing line? Kept it small? For just herself, as a hobby? But she knew that it had not been a mistake how big things had gotten for her.

She always knew that she had a gift—that she'd do something great with her talent one day. It was a small miracle that she'd ever even let herself dream that big, given the circumstances of the crappy life she'd grown up in. Was Jemma the same? Were there dreams yet to be realized by the young girl or in Blu's quest to help her—to save her from a bad life, had she done more harm than good?

Blu let herself drift off to sleep for a few minutes, noting that the noise down the hall had stopped and hoping that Jemma was also getting some much-needed rest. She'd speak with her when she woke up. She'd make her understand how much Blu loved her and beg her to trust that she knew what was best for her.

Blu looked at the clock next to her, for a moment forgetting the disaster that had taken place that day. She'd been asleep for only fifteen minutes, but she did feel a lot better now that she'd had a little rest. It was time to go check on Jemma.

She knocked on Jemma's door and, after getting no answer, opened it quietly. Thinking that she must have already gone downstairs, Blu turned to make her way down to speak with her. She'd suggest that they order pizza and have a movie night, and soon things would be back to normal. That worked when Jemma was five, she thought and willed herself to go into the conversation with a positive attitude.

Before Blu had a chance to make it to the living room, where she assumed she'd find Jemma on the sofa watching TV or playing one of her video games, she spotted the note on the kitchen counter.

Dear Mom,

I've gone back to meet my grandma. You can't stop me.

Jemma

The simple note in the childlike scrawl made Blu's

heart beat wildly in her chest. Panicked, she grabbed her keys and ran upstairs to get her phone, ringing Chase as she made her way back to her car. Please pick up. Please pick up. But it went straight to voicemail again. She took a moment to catch her breath, thinking about where Jemma would be, before she backed out of the driveway without a plan.

The bus. For sure she'd thought that she could take the bus back. She felt good and then panic-stricken as well, thinking about the area where the bus stop was near the motel. It was not a place for young girls. Blu drove to the stop near her house as quickly as she could, hoping that Jemma had left not long before and might still be waiting for the bus. But there was no one there.

Blu was crying now, trying to think clearly about what that particular bus route might be and how long Jemma would be on it. God, please keep her safe. She realized that she had to phone her mother now. She didn't dwell on it as she waited for her to pick up, willing her to pick up.

"Hello, Blu?" She answered on the third ring, her voice sounding hopeful.

"Hi, I—I need your help." Blu was crying into the phone.

"What is it? What's wrong? Are you okay?" Her mom was panicking now on the other end.

"It's Jemma. She's left me a note that she's coming to see you. I'm sure she's taking the bus, but she's—she's never taken it alone before and God, if something happens to her…" Blu was crying into the phone. She could hear her mom's door shutting in the background.

"I'm heading out the door now to walk to the bus stop. Don't worry. She's gonna be okay."

Blu willed it to be true, that by chance there'd be no weirdos on the bus that day, that Jemma would remember where the right stop was, that everything would be okay. God, why didn't I give Jemma the phone that she's been wanting? She made a mental note to do so now as a matter of necessity, wishing so much that she could call her now, that Jemma had a way to reach out to her if she was in trouble.

"Please stay on the phone with me. I'm driving on the freeway now. I'd follow the bus route, but I have no idea what that is," she cried out to her mother on the other end of the line. "I'll be there in ten minutes." It was a stretch and it meant speeding, but Blu didn't care about that right now. She needed to get to Jemma.

Ten minutes or so later, she hung up the phone after telling her mom she was at the exit and would be there in a minute. As she pulled up to where her mom was waiting by the bus stop she saw the bus just beyond, in the near distance. It's just pulled away from the stop. Blu was about to drive past her mom to catch up with the bus, when she realized that her mom was waving for her to pull over. Blu rolled down the window, yelling to her in one breath, "We have to go catch that bus."

"No, no." Her mom was opening the car door and motioning for Blu to turn around on the street. "The bus stopped and when she didn't get off, I went on to speak with the driver and check. He said that a young girl had gotten off a few stops back. I'm pretty sure that if we just turn around, that's just up this street."

Jemma, please still be on this same street. She was picturing the young girl scared and wandering around by herself trying to remember where the motel was.

CHAPTER 25

Blu was trying to keep it together when her mom got in the car. What if Jemma had wandered off, gotten lost? She'd never forgive herself for starting this mess with her mom—she'd never forgive her mother.

Blu glared at her mom sitting next to her in the car. "I'm so angry that I ever listened to you—ever believed you. Look what's happened. If something happens to her, I'll never forgive you."

Her mother looked liked she was trying to keep it together, crying quiet tears as she allowed Blu to rant.

"We'll find her. I'm sure she'd just gonna be right up here a little further."

They were both studying the sidewalks on either side of the road carefully, but so far there was no glimpse of the young girl.

"Okay, she's not on this main road." God, why didn't I give Jemma that phone? "I think we should start looking down some of the side streets. She probably realized that she'd gotten off at the wrong stop and figured she'd try to walk to the motel." Blu took a deep breath and looked at her mom. "She's never taken this bus by herself before."

Her mom reached out to take her hand and Blu snatched it away. She was trying to put her anger aside but she was a bomb waiting to explode. *Just keep it together until you find her. Yelling and screaming right now is not gonna help find Jemma.*

Blu turned the car to check out another street, getting further and further from the main one where the bus would have let Jemma off. She was growing more panicked by the minute.

Her mother was pointing. "There. There she is."

In the distance, Blu saw her, looking upset, sitting on the curb, her head in her hands.

Blu started honking the horn, feeling shocked and relieved. She saw Jemma look up, getting quickly to her feet, a look of relief apparent on her face. Blu pulled the car over to the side of the road, not bothering to turn it off as she jumped out to run to Jemma, who was flying into her arms in a matter of seconds.

"I'm so sorry, Mom." Jemma was sobbing, clinging to Blu's neck. "I thought I knew how to get there on the bus, but I got lost."

Blu hugged her tight, stroking her hair. "Shh, it's okay."

They started walking towards the car, Jemma still in tears.

"I just wanted to see her—my grandma." Jemma

stopped suddenly, looking towards the car.

In the rush of finding Jemma, Blu had somehow forgotten all about her mom being there, and now she was standing next to the passenger door, looking timid, but smiling widely at Jemma. Blu looked at her intently before she spoke, trying to communicate with her face how the conversation would go.

Jemma walked up to Blu's mom with a shy smile beginning on her face.

"Jemma, this is your grandma," Blu said and her mom nodded.

"Hi, Jemma. It's nice to meet you." She held out her hand to the child.

Jemma, never one for being shy, rushed forward towards her grandma, arms hugging her around the waist, pressing her face against her chest. "Hi."

Blu's mom squeezed her tight for a moment, then backed off slightly to hold her at arm's length. "My, aren't you lovely."

"Thank you," Jemma said. "It's so great to finally meet you."

Blu was making her way around the car to the driver's seat, feeling like she couldn't breathe. Just keep it together a little while longer. She didn't want to say or do anything in front of Jemma, but inside her blood was boiling.

"Alright then, let's get in the car. I'll take you back to the motel," she said to her mother, willing her to not say anything.

Her mother nodded silently.

"I want to do something with Grandma," Jemma said from the backseat. "Can't we go for dinner or something?"

"Not now, Jemma," Blu said, her face stern and her heart beating wildly.

"But Mom, I—"

"Jemma, I said not now."

Jemma sulked in the back of the car while Blu drove the few blocks to the motel in silence. Her mom sat looking out the window, her face turned away and unreadable to Blu.

Blu's mind was racing. She had to end this once and for all. Get her mother out of their lives for good. It wasn't going to be easy now with Jemma. The fact that she'd already met her grandma was going to make it that much harder to explain anything to her that would make sense. And she wasn't ready for the truth. It was way too soon for that.

Blu pulled the car up to the motel parking lot and turned off the ignition. She grabbed her purse from the backseat, looking at Jemma as she did so. "Stay here," she ordered. To her mother, "Let me walk you inside."

"But Mom, no. I wanna come too." Jemma was already outside of the car and around to where her grandma had gotten out.

Blu took a deep breath and shouted. "Jemma, please listen to me."

Jemma looked at her, her eyes wide at the tone of her mother's voice, which Blu knew was getting increasingly more agitated.

"Give your grandma a hug goodbye and then I want you to wait for me in the car."

Jemma looked at her with defiance on her face for a few seconds, before she finally put her arms around her grandmother's waist again, letting the woman squeeze her tight before untangling her arms from her waist.

Blu's mother looked at her, while Blu waited impatiently for them to finish.

"Go on now, Jemma. Listen to your mother," she said, throwing a look in Blu's direction as if to let her know that she was trying.

Jemma gave one last squeeze and then stomped back around to the other side of the car.

"Lock the door and stay here. I'll be back in a few minutes," Blu said, completely out of patience and just wanting to get this whole thing over with.

She motioned for her mother to start towards her motel room. "I'll be right there."

Blu's mother started walking away, and Blu saw her look back one last time at Jemma before she got into the car.

Blu waited until after Jemma had climbed into the backseat, shutting the door with a loud slam and clicking the lock as she glared at her mother.

She turned to make her way to the motel room then,

each step more determined than the last, her hand in her purse, ready to make this final.

She barely glanced at her mother as she entered the room and made her way to the small table in the corner, whipping out her checkbook and grabbing the pen that she found in the table drawer.

Her mother sat on the edge of the bed watching her, and Blu couldn't help but wonder if she was thinking about how sly she'd been making this trip, about how she'd gone about it and how everything would end up working out just the way she had planned.

Blu gritted her teeth, the pen poised above the check she was writing. What would it take? What was the magic number? She knew, even as she was writing it, that it was way more than her mother would have ever asked for—an amount of money that would solve any problem that her mother could have. It would do it—seal the deal. Blu was sure of it as she ripped the check out, stood up and walked over to where her mother sat.

Blu handed the check to her, determined to say what she had to say, walk out, and never see the woman again.

Her mother looked down at the check and back up at Blu with a question on her face. "What—"

"This should be more than enough money to fix any problems that you might have," Blu said, cutting her off.

"Blu, I—I don't want your money." She handed the check back towards her daughter.

Blu pushed her hand away. "Take the money. All I

ask is that you stay out of our lives for good." She felt her face pinch, her heart beat as she worked hard to get her point across. Don't you get it? I don't want this. I don't want you. I—we don't need you.

"Blu, there's been a terrible misunderstanding. Harold—all of this. What I told you the other day was true. And I don't want your money. I never wanted anything from you. I was being honest with you when I told you that during our first meeting." Her mother was crying hard now, tears rushing down her face, pleading with Blu. "Please, you have to believe me—to give me a chance to show you."

Blu felt her resolve weakening just the tiniest bit as she looked at her mother, crumpling before her—at least appearing to be heartbroken. God, she really did want to believe her. Why did she want it so badly? They'd been fine without her all these years. But as she looked out the only window of the small motel room towards Jemma sitting alone in the car, she knew that she was making the right decision.

"Please, Blu."

Her mom was still trying to make her understand, but there was no use prolonging it a moment longer. She still had Jemma to deal with, and it was going to be a long night.

She stood in front of her mother to say what she knew would be her final words to her.

"Jemma is my whole life. She has been since the day

she was born. Since the day I took her away from you to make a better life for her. I love that child as if she were my own daughter."

Blu's mother was sobbing on the bed, and Blu was brushing at the tears that threatened to stream down her own face as she went on.

"But she's my daughter, Blu." Her mother said the words quietly, as if she was trying to convince herself of it more than Blu.

There was silence in the room. There it was. Blu gulped, the fear threatening to overtake even the intense rage she was feeling now.

"You say that you understand what I did, that you want the best for me—for Jemma." She looked at her mother, waiting for the acknowledgement that came with a nod of her head.

"I do," she said, crying and Blu knew that she wanted to say more but her mother seemed to shrink before her, the earlier truth of her words disappearing in an invisible cloud of guilt surrounding her as she waited for Blu to finish.

"If you really mean that. If you really love her—" She looked intently at her mother, who was still crying and seemingly pleading her with her eyes to stop. "—then you'll take this check, go away from here, and leave us both alone."

It wasn't a question really and Blu didn't wait for an answer. "I never want to hear from you again." She waited for the slow nod of her mother's head before she walked out the door of the motel room, not looking back until she was in the car, turning it around to head towards home.

Blu turned her head slightly to see her mother standing in the window of her room, her hand raised in a wave towards the car, her face plastered in what Blu knew was a smile just for Jemma. She caught a glimpse of Jemma in the rearview window crying, her face pressed against the window of the car as she waved towards her grandma. You'll never know that she's your mother, Blu thought, as she drove away more determined than ever that the past was behind them now for good.

CHAPTER 26

Blu drove away from her mother in silence. There were things to be said, but Blu was so angry and Jemma still looked so upset that she didn't think speaking about it now would do either of them any good. She caught a glimpse of Jemma looking out the backseat window, tears still streaming as she wiped them away roughly. She's tough like I was at her age. Blu's heart plummeted as she had the thought. She'd tried so hard to raise a little girl who would be happy, have a happy life. But there was nothing about Jemma now that conveyed anything but a deep sorrow. Blu would make her understand one day. She knew she was doing the right thing by her.

Then why was she suddenly having such doubts about it? Her greatest fear was that Jemma would hate her one day when she found out the truth about her—when she found out that Blu was not her real mother.

Jemma looked away from the window now and Blu could see her staring intently at her from the backseat.

"I hate you," she said quietly, but with such venom in her voice, it shocked Blu.

"Honey. I'm so sorry. I know this doesn't make a lot

of sense right now but—"

"It makes no sense. I don't understand what the big deal is, what my grandma did that was so bad?"

Blu got the sense that Jemma was calming down just a bit, wanting answers now. She pulled in the driveway, turned off the car, and twisted in her seat in order to look the child in the face. "Honey, there are things about your grandma—and—and that man we saw there earlier today—"

"Who was that?" Jemma interrupted. "Was that my grandfather?"

That lowlife is your father.

"No, Jemma, he's not. He's just—he's a bad guy that your grandma can't seem to get out of her life. The two of them together don't do well. And I don't want you around that—around them."

Jemma was silent.

"Can you understand that?"

More silence from the young girl.

"Jemma, please look at me."

She obeyed, turning her tear-stained face towards Blu.

"Honey, can you just trust me with this?"

Jemma looked like she was deep in thought for a minute before she spoke. "Is it okay if I think that you're wrong?"

Blu smiled, despite the grim conversation. "Yes. It's okay if you don't agree with me, but—" She wanted to be sure that she had her full attention. "You have to promise me that you're never gonna pull what you pulled today—taking off like that by yourself. That was not okay at all."

Jemma looked down. Blu knew that she was well aware that she'd be in trouble for her actions earlier. She looked at her mom and nodded her head. "I know. I won't do it again."

"Okay, good, now that we have that settled, you are also grounded—"

"Mom, no!"

"Yes, for two weeks, and you're lucky it's not for a whole month." Blu was firm; she knew that Jemma would know better than to argue with her about the punishment.

Jemma didn't say another word as she got out of the car, slamming the door behind her. Blu followed her into the house as she stomped up to her room, giving a weird sense of déjà vu to the whole scene for a second time that day.

This time I am parking myself downstairs, Blu thought, as she went to the kitchen to make herself a cup of tea.

She called Jemma on the intercom. "Shall I order us a pizza?" An olive branch to the young girl. She waited for several seconds. "Jemma?"

"Okay, sure."

Blu took a deep breath. Jemma will be okay. She will. "Okay, I'll call you when it's here."

She took her tea and her phone over to the breakfast table. God, the day I've had. She really needed to be with

Chase, but she knew he was working tonight. She sent him a text, trying to say in as few words as possible everything that had happened to her today—but more importantly letting him know that she needed him.

She smiled when her phone dinged right away with his text back.

God, babe. Sounds like an awful day. Do you want me to come over late to spend the night? I promise I'll sneak out before Jemma wakes up. I love you.

Blu smiled. Yes, that was exactly what she wanted—what she needed.

Yes, please. I love you too.

She had made such huge strides recently when it came to trust. First with Chase, then opening up to her mother—to the idea of letting her into her life again. That had been a mistake, and it had made her doubt herself once again. How could she have been so wrong about how she was feeling? The thought irritated her because she'd always been someone who wasn't run by her feelings. It was what had caused her walls to form, but for good reason, she knew.

But even after everything that had just happened, she knew that she had turned some corners, knowing that her trust in Chase was different. It was earned, and she'd not let him down by allowing those same walls to go up and hurt their relationship, the strides that they'd made in being open with one another. He was worth more than that to her. And he kept showing her over and over again what his love for her was like. It felt complete in a way that Blu hadn't been loved before. She was incredibly grateful that after the pain of the day, she'd have Chase's arms to settle into that night. He'd make it seem less awful than it was, and she'd allow him to help her to feel better.

CHAPTER 27

The next couple of months flew by as Blu settled back into her work, making some real progress finally with the latest designs that she had to have ready for the upcoming European shows. Jemma was doing well in school; but there was a constant nagging thought in Blu's mind that she really needed to start doing some planning for her upcoming travel and how that would affect Jemma.

Chase nearly had her convinced that she needed to sign up with a local agency and let them find someone who could act as both nanny and tutor, allowing her to take Jemma away with her. Well, it wasn't really a question of not doing so. Blu would never leave Jemma behind without her for that length of time. It was just that she was dragging her feet because she'd always been so resistant to having outside help in general when it came to Jemma.

Thinking about Chase made her smile. He hadn't moved in yet—they weren't quite ready for that step, or rather she wasn't quite ready for it—but he spent the night several times during any given week, and half the time he was there in the morning making breakfast when Jemma woke up. So really her reluctance over the change that moving in together would mean had more to do with how Jemma might feel about it; but in reality Blu knew that Jemma loved Chase as much as she herself did, and she suspected there wouldn't be much resistance to the idea.

She looked up from her desk when she heard the light tap of a knock from the open door, grinning before she saw Chase's face. She'd given him a key a few weeks ago, and he'd surprised her on several early-afternoon occasions by turning up for a little alone time before Jemma arrived home from school.

He crossed the room to bend down and give her a warm kiss on the lips before flopping onto the comfy couch against the wall. Sometimes he'd sit there for hours while she worked, content to listen to music and stare out at the ocean. He said that the sound of her sewing machine relaxed him, which made her incredibly happy. Today, though, she was busy on her laptop, her latest designs put away while she worked on getting her finances in order for the month. She kept vowing to hire someone to help her with it, as it really wasn't something she enjoyed very much; ironically, the vast increase in her bank account hadn't changed this fact over the past few years.

"What are you doing?" Chase asked as he lay back against the sofa cushion to study her.

"Oh, you know—balancing my bank statement, paying bills—all that fun stuff that I love so much."

They both laughed, knowing that nothing was further from the truth than that statement.

"Hmm."

"What's hmm? Forgot about one of your many shopping sprees?" Another statement that was completely ironic, because Blu rarely spent big amounts of money on herself, unless it was absolutely necessary. Chase blew her a kiss, teasing her as he waited for her reply. He was constantly trying to get her to treat herself or to learn to graciously accept the many lavish gifts that he liked to buy for her.

"So it's another month that's gone by that my mother's not cashed the check." She looked in her checkbook as if she had to double-check that her spoken statement was true, even though she'd been checking her bank records online every day after the first month that the check hadn't been cashed. She shut her checkbook and walked over to snuggle in next to Chase on the small sofa, enjoying the feel of his arm coming around her, pulling her close in a way that she'd grown very used to.

"And what are you thinking about this?" Chase lowered his face to kiss her on the top of the head.

"I dunno exactly what to think," Blu said, not quite sure if she was willing to get into a big discussion about it, but knowing that Chase could help her to wade through her own emotions, as he always had a way of doing.

"What do you think it means?"

Chase was quiet for a moment, always thoughtful with his opinions and advice, a trait Blu had come to really appreciate about him. "How long has it been? Since you gave her the check?"

Blu already knew the answer—to the day. "It's been two months and five days."

Chase tilted her face up to meet his eyes. "I think it means that your mother is not going to cash that check."

Hearing someone else say it out loud caused the little glimmer of hope that she'd been nursing somewhere deep inside to flutter to the surface. Dare she think it?

"But why? Why wouldn't she cash it?" She was voicing the question out loud but it had been in her head for days; over and over it played in her mind, begging for an answer. She sat up now, pulling herself away from Chase so that she could see his face.

He leaned over to kiss her quickly on the lips. "Maybe because what she told you about not wanting money from you was the truth?"

"But then what else does that mean, Chase?" She was trying to wrap her head around the idea that if she was wrong about the money, then might she have been wrong about everything?

"Honey, I think it might mean that your mom was being genuine about just wanting to get to know you."

"But what about Harold—I mean, I know what I saw and I definitely saw him at her motel. Do you really think it would be that much of a coincidence that he just showed up here at the same time?"

Chase was quiet for a few seconds, considering her question. "Well, it's quite possible that he saw you on TV also and figured out the rest for himself—in terms of following your mom here. I mean, from what you said, she told you about him trying to contact her once in awhile; that's not a crazy idea, is it?"

"No. I suppose not." Blu was quiet as she thought back to that last conversation with her mother. She had been very adamant that it was over between her and Harold—that she never wanted anything to do with him again. She'd been adamant about a lot of things during that last day, and Blu had been so enraged that she didn't bother to seriously consider that anything she was saying wasn't a lie. But now—the fact that her mother hadn't cashed the check—it was all weighing heavily on her.

"Chase?"

"Yeah, babe?"

"What do you think I should do?" She needed someone to tell her—to give her permission to let the walls come down again.

Chase pulled her back over into his arms. "I think maybe you need to listen to your instinct on this." He winked at her.

He knew her very well already, she thought, smiling.

"Okay, so let's say that I was wrong—that she had been telling the truth the whole time. Don't you think she would have tried to call me by now? Email me? Something?"

Chase was looking at her with a funny expression on his face.

"What?" Blu asked.

"Honey, I've seen you angry before." He was teasing her, but she had the feeling he was about to make a good point. "From the way you described your last conversation with her—so angry, and telling her what she ought to do if she really loved you and Jemma—well, I mean, isn't she doing what you asked of her?"

Blu nodded.

"I mean she probably does feel incredible guilt, even though you know that she's trying to work through all that. I'm sure it took a lot for her to even come here—to imagine that you might allow her back into your life—into Jemma's life again. Your words to her probably reinforced her own doubts, I'd imagine."

"Hmm."

"What's hmm now?" Chased teased, nuzzling her neck with his lips.

"I think maybe I've made a mistake," Blu said quietly. She disentangled herself from Chase's arms once more to sit up and look at him. "The question is, what do I do about it? How do I find out the truth? And what if I'm getting my hopes up all over again and it turns out there's a perfectly good explanation for why the greedy woman hasn't cashed my check yet?" She laughed but she was serious about her own doubts too.

"What if?" Chase was saying. "Then you'll come to me and I'll help you to feel better all over again." He smiled. "Wanna know what I really think you should do?"

"Yes." Blu said quickly. "I do."

"I think you should go there—to your mom's."

Blu's eyes widened as he continued. "When?"

"Soon. As soon as you can. Before you change your mind." He wasn't laughing or teasing her. There was something serious about his words.

"Chase? Are you serious right now? Does that even sound like me?" She was shaking her head in answer to her own question. "I mean, if anything, I was thinking of maybe giving her a call."

"Blu." He was looking her in the eye intently.

She nodded in acknowledgment.

"That's kind of my point."

Blu looked at him, with an idea of where he was going with this.

"I just think that maybe a little leap of faith might be required here—trusting yourself, but more importantly being willing to just go for it, knowing that you're going to come back home to Jemma—to me—and be fine regardless of what happens." He looked her in the eye again. "And I just—I just think this thing with your mom is important. Like, really important."

Blu felt tears coming to her eyes as she leaned in to give him a big hug, her voice catching on the sob that caught her by surprise. "You're right. It is important."

CHAPTER 28

Blu's stomach was in knots during the entire plane ride to New York. She'd hired a driver to pick her up so that she could go straight to her mom's place north of the city. She was taking a huge risk that her mom would even be home, but during their earlier conversations, she'd found out that she was still living in the same small house that they'd lived in when Blu was fifteen.

She remembered the day that her mom had told her they were moving. It was during a period that her mother had been doing better. She'd completed a few months of rehab and kicked Harold out. The outpatient program she was in helped her with securing a job and getting her into a small house. It wasn't the best neighborhood, but at the time Blu was extremely happy to finally be getting out of the trailer park which had held nothing but bad memories. It was a fresh start for her and her mother.

The two-hour drive from the airport to her mother's passed quickly, with Blu deep in thought. What am I really hoping to accomplish by being here? She'd second-guessed herself so many times, but the nagging doubt continued to plague her. She'd never be able to really move on until she got these last answers. What she hoped to find and what she expected to find were two totally different things, and she was continually forcing herself to push both thoughts out of her head and just remind herself that this trip was about closure for her—and on behalf of Jemma. She needed to feel confident for Jemma's sake that she hadn't made a mistake.

They pulled up to the address that Blu had given the driver. The run-down neighborhood looked oddly the same, and looking at the small house brought back a flash of memory to the day they'd moved in. It had been a quick move, with the few pieces of furniture that they'd had. One of her mom's friends had helped pile it into the back of his pick-up truck, and the whole thing took about ninety minutes.

What Blu remembered about that day was the picnic they'd had on the floor in the middle of the small living room—their small living room. Her mom's friend had left, and with a huge grin on her face, her mom had said that they were going to celebrate their new life together. She ordered a pizza, which was a rare treat for Blu, spread out a blanket on the living room floor, and turned up the oldies rock station on the radio real loud—they didn't have to worry as much about the noise as they had in the trailer. And there was dancing—a lot of silly dancing until the pizza arrived. Blu smiled at the memory of her mother.

Everything was good for about two months. Then Harold convinced her mom to take him back and within days she'd relapsed again. Before the end of that year, Blu had left for good. On her own at the age of sixteen. And she'd been on her own ever since then.

She flashed to Chase and the little family of friends that she loved so much. But she wasn't alone any more. And there was no reason to believe that she ever would be again. She'd found something that she hadn't even realized was lacking in her and Jemma's lives. So this closure with her mom wasn't so much about that. It was coming from a place of strength on Blu's part, not weakness—not from needing her in any way. But she wanted it, if she was being honest. She hadn't allowed herself to even imagine a relationship with her mother until these past few months, but once she did, she couldn't stop thinking about the possibility. A new life with her mother, and possibly for her mother. But she was getting ahead of herself with her thoughts now.

She sat in the car for a few moments, taking in the surroundings, drawing in the deep breath that she needed to make the trip up the narrow walkway to the front door. The house needed a fresh coat of paint and the yard looked like it hadn't been mowed in months. She noticed that there wasn't a car in the parking spot next to the house, which probably meant that no one would be here anyways. If that were true, she wasn't even sure what her next move would be—how long she'd stay in town or how many attempts she'd make to come by. She only knew that she had to try.

Blu slowly walked up onto the front porch, for the first time noticing the piece of paper taped to the front door. She took a deep breath and tapped lightly on the door. When she couldn't hear anyone coming after several seconds, she knocked again, louder this time. She saw the curtain in the window next to the door flutter slightly, and then the door opened.

"Blu?" Her mother's expression was that of shock. "Hi. Wow. What are you doing here? I—I mean, come in."

It was a natural response to invite her in, Blu knew. But she also noticed that her mom seemed slightly uneasy after Blu had stepped through the door.

"I'm sorry for not calling—for not warning you that I was coming," Blu said, wishing it were true that she hadn't showed up unannounced on purpose, that she hadn't wanted to give her mom a chance to hide anything—to prepare for Blu's arrival. *I need to know the truth.*

"Sit down." Her mom was gesturing towards the same worn-out sofa that Blu remembered from her teenage years. "Can I get you something to drink? I've got a pot of coffee on already."

Blu nodded. "Yes, a cup of coffee would be great, thanks."

She took in her surroundings quickly as her mom retreated to the kitchen. The interior of the small house was just as she remembered. Everything was the same in regards to the furniture. Maybe one chair in the corner was different, and the old black-and-white TV that had never worked had been replaced with a small flat-screened version. There were more books on the bookshelf, and she couldn't help but smile when she noticed the black-and-white picture of her grandparents, who had passed away when she was a baby. The framed photo was still in the same spot, hanging on the wall in the corner of the room.

Her mother returned with two coffees, and Blu noticed her hand shaking as she set the tray down on the coffee table in front of them, before seating herself on the sofa next to Blu.

"I just can't get over that you're here," she said.

Blu noticed that she was fidgeting with her hands like she didn't quite know what to do with them. It's no wonder that she would be nervous to see me after the last time that I spoke to her, Blu thought, while at the same time realizing that she needed to put her out of her misery, letting her know why she had come. She turned her body towards her mother on the sofa, meeting her eyes as she spoke.

"Why haven't you cashed the check I gave you?" Blu said evenly.

Her mother sat up a little straighter on the sofa,

squaring her shoulders—Putting on her own invisible armor, Blu thought—her eyes returning the intensity of Blu's stare.

"I meant it when I told you that I didn't want your money. I won't cash that check. You can take it back or we can rip it up here and now. I don't want it and I don't need it, Blu."

Blu looked at her, neither of them speaking for a full minute.

Finally Blu spoke. "What about the eviction notice on your door?"

"I told you that I still have some things to work out—that being one of them."

Blu wasn't sure what the look was that passed on her mother's face, but it briefly reminded her of herself—of a position that she'd been in before, that of needing help, but not being willing to take it. But you didn't offer any help to her, you offered your mother a bribe—one which she obviously didn't take. The thought crossed her mind as she continued to eye her mother thoughtfully.

"Okay." Finally Blu spoke again. "Are you going to be able to do that—to keep your house?" It was none of her business. She knew this as she asked but couldn't help herself.

Her mother sighed. "I'll figure it out, Blu. I will. It's nothing for you to worry about."

Blu looked down, all at once feeling embarrassed and unsure how to continue the conversation. "But, why—

why wouldn't you take the money? It seems as though you could really use it." It was a stupid thing to say but she couldn't resist. She had to hear it again from her mother's mouth.

Her mother looked thoughtful—and proud, Blu thought—for a few moments before she spoke again.

"Blu, when I came to see you, I never wanted anything from you, especially not your money. I can keep telling you and you can choose to believe it or not, but it's just the truth." Blu was nodding her head, encouraging her to continue. "I used the bit of money that I had saved to pay for that plane ticket and my stay in the motel. All of that was worth it to me to see you—to try to make you understand why I was there."

Blu had been wrong about her mom. She felt it now deep in her gut. She believed her, but she didn't stop her as she continued.

"I know that I've made a lot of mistakes in my lifetime. Too many to count, and the most critical ones being losing you and Jemma. I'll never forgive myself for that, but all I can do is keep working my program to stay sober and better my life. It's all I have now and that's okay with me. It just has to be." She looked down, taking in a deep breath. "Because the moment I give up is the moment that my life will really be over, and I'm not willing to become another sad statistic. I really did make a decision to change, and I won't stop until I'm on my feet."

Blu felt the tears stinging her eyes as she tried to get the words out past the lump in her throat. She had to be sure. "And Harold?"

"He's gone, Blu. He really isn't in my life. I know it seems hard to believe, but the fact that he tracked me down, following me to San Diego, was a total fluke that I had nothing to do with. And yes, he was interested in what he could get from you after he saw your interview on TV." Her mother stood up from the sofa then, appearing to gather more strength from each word that she spoke. "I really don't know what else to tell you about him, except it's over between us—there's no part of me that wants him back in my life." She looked at Blu then with a look that reminded her of Jemma—a pure look of defiance—and it was all Blu could do to keep from smiling.

This woman standing before her now was not someone that she'd ever known before—this was a fighter, unlike any Blu had ever seen in this home. Gone was the sick, helpless woman that Blu had known strung out on drugs so long ago. Gone even was the woman that Blu had met two months earlier, eager to win her approval, to seek her forgiveness. No, this woman standing in front of her now was not apologizing for her past or her future. She was not apologizing for who she was, and the impact of her speech was overwhelming to Blu in a way that moved her to her core.

Blu stood up, wiping her sudden tears away, and

reached for her mother, who willingly moved into her embrace. Blu squeezed her tight, both of them hugging in silence as Blu collected the many thoughts running wild in her brain.

Finally she pulled away slightly to look her mother in the eye, both women crying silent tears, both overwhelmed by what was happening between them.

"Mom, I believe you." Blu said it quietly and watched her mom crumple to the sofa as new sobs overtook her. "I'm sorry for what I've put you through—"

"No, no. It's I who am—"

"No, you've apologized enough." Her mother looked at her through her tears and Blu sat next to her on the sofa, taking her hand in her own as she continued speaking quietly. "I'm so—so proud of you—for what you've done." Her mother looked at her and Blu recognized the hope in her eyes—the same hope that she herself had known over the years. Blu nodded her head and grabbed her mother again for a hug, her voice barely more than a whisper. "I'm going to help you—" She pulled away to look her in the eyes again. "—if you'll let me.

Blu's mother nodded her head slowly, followed by a smile that Blu believed signified gratefulness for the life raft that her daughter was throwing her. They were done now—done being on opposite sides of the fight, trying to convince each other of the motives that were, in fact, honest and pure. Her mother's, to know the daughter that she'd lost so long ago; and Blu's, to help the mother who deserved a second chance at life. Both had much to gain, both were now willing to take the risk that was so worth it.

Blu imagined it was a lot for her mother to take in—it was for her too. She didn't really know what she'd expected in coming here, but she didn't expect to feel so sure so fast. And she wasn't doubting herself for a second. She wouldn't do that to her mother again.

The two women sat hugging for a few moments in silence. Finally Blu spoke. "I'll book a room nearby and we'll spend some time together over the next few days to see what we need to sort out for you with the house—with everything."

Her mother nodded but looked like she wanted to say something.

"What is it?" Bu asked.

"Do you—would you want to stay here? I mean, I know it's not—"

"Yes." Blu grinned. "It will be perfect—and I have an idea for dinner—my treat."

CHAPTER 29

Blu sat on a blanket on the floor with her mom, eating pizza and laughing as they chatted. Music was playing in the background, and she'd traded the soda of her memories for a bottle of sparkling cider that she'd picked up at the shop down the road. Her mom looked so happy—as happy as Blu was feeling in the moment, to be here with her. It felt totally carefree and completely different than any time they'd spent together in California a few months earlier.

"Do you remember when we first moved into this house—we had a pizza party like this, just the two of us," Blu said, feeling an odd sense of traveling full circle.

Her mom nodded her head slowly. "I do, but only vaguely."

Blu thought she sounded sad and didn't really want to ruin the mood. "It was a happy time—one of the happiest I can remember—dancing here with you, talking about the future in our new house."

"Unfortunately, any great memories that I had have

seemed to get clouded over by the drug-induced brain fog that I created shortly after them." Her mom sighed. "I do have a lot of regrets, Blu. I want you to know that—that I wish I could go back and change the past—be a real mom to you—and to Jemma."

"I do know that." Blu smiled and reached out to take her mom's hand. "But like you said earlier, it's about focusing on change for you, making your life better now. And you are doing that."

Her mom nodded her head, brushing away a few tears. "Yes, I know. I keep telling myself that I can't live in the past. I have to forgive myself and move on. It's just that some days doing that is easier than other days."

Blu waited a moment to respond, looking at her mom, thinking about how far they'd come in such a short while. "I do want you to know that I forgive you. I really mean that." And she did—and in doing so, she felt the burden lift within herself.

Her mother looked at her with new tears forming in her eyes as she reached out to hug her daughter. "You don't know what that means to me—it means everything."

Blu nodded and raised her glass of cider. "To new beginnings—for both of us."

With a wide smile, her mom raised her glass. "Cheers to that."

It was strange sleeping in her old room, much of it

just as she'd remembered it. Thankfully most of her worst memories of Harold were from the trailer. By the time Blu had turned fifteen and was living in this house, he'd not dared to visit her bedroom at night. She was much too feisty at that age—she'd been sleeping with a knife under her pillow for two years by that time.

It was incredible, really, to think of how much her life had changed—where she was living now and the kinds of things that money could buy. She was of the opinion that money didn't buy you happiness, but she had come to realize was that it did, in fact, buy you security—and not just the financial kind.

She remembered the early days with Jemma, when she'd first moved to San Francisco and could barely afford a small studio apartment in one of the worst parts of town. Those times had been tough, and she'd worked hard to always be sure that Jemma felt safe and protected by her.

The sirens outside down the street reminded her that not a lot had changed for her mother in that regard. She'd guessed that her mom's greatest worry was about money, and tomorrow they were going to sit down and talk about what needed to be paid—the financial pieces that Blu could help her with—and she was glad to do it. Unlike when she'd written her the huge check, her heart full of fear and determination to keep her away, this time the money wasn't a payoff.

Blu thought about the phone conversation that she'd

had with Chase earlier, filling him in on everything that had happened. He'd been so genuinely pleased for her, listening to her as she talked about possible solutions to helping her mother out, offering her his own insights and giving her a lot to think about by the time they'd hung up. She was so thankful that Chase had talked her into coming here, recognizing her need for closure and perhaps trusting his own instinct that she'd been wrong about her mother.

She smiled as she thought about her mother and spending the next few days with her. It was so nice to be able to do that without the strain that had been there during the attempt a few months ago. It felt more honest now, largely due to Blu's own doubts being cast aside. She imagined that it could be tough for her mother to share her financial burdens with her, but Blu would do her best to help her to feel like it wasn't a big deal, which reminded her that she needed to share more about her own past—and Arianna—with her. She'd told her a little bit about the best friend that she'd had but there was a lot still to be told. Blu thought that it would help her mother to accept the financial help from her, so it all needed to be said. She couldn't help but laugh a little bit as she thought about what Arianna would have thought about the situation—that Blu was using Arianna's money to help her mother. She would have loved that.

Blu sat with her mom at her kitchen table, bills and

file folders of information spread out in front of them. She knew that it hadn't been easy for her, but finally her mother had just agreed to let Blu look at all of it.

"It's a mess." Her mother looked overwhelmed as she placed the stack of bills down on the table. "You know, the one thing about being strung out on drugs is that you really don't give yourself any space to care about things such as finances and paying bills. I don't know how I ever survived as long as I did, to be honest."

Blu nodded and hoped that her mother would see that she was trying to be supportive and not judgmental as the questions came forth.

"How have you been doing it—paying everything—until now, I mean?"

"I took some classes that were offered in the program that I was in after rehab. One of them was in personal finance, so actually I've come a long ways since the pre-sober days." She laughed. "Harold had been keeping a job for several years, so he was taking care of the house payments and a few of the other big bills before he left."

"And are you working—right now, I mean?" Blu asked carefully, as it was a topic that hadn't been brought up at all between them. When she was younger, her mom was constantly bouncing between odd jobs waitressing and house cleaning, and then anything that would bring in a little money after she'd lost one of the other jobs. Blu, herself, used to contribute some of her babysitting money to help pay the bills—her mother had seen to it that she knew that it was part of her job to help take care of the family. Blu hadn't really resented it too much back then. She didn't know any different, and was determined that they didn't end up on the street.

"I'd been working for the past two years at a restaurant across town. It was a great job with really good tips and they let me work a lot of extra shifts, so it hasn't been a problem paying the bills until I was let go—a few months ago." She looked down as if she was suddenly ashamed.

"A few months ago? So, before you came out to San Diego?" Blu said carefully.

"Yes, I know it probably wasn't wise, but I just needed to do it. I really thought that I'd be able to find a job when I came back, but it's been a lot harder than I thought it would be."

And the house?" Blu asked.

"When I lost the job, I knew I was going to have a problem keeping the house, so I decided to quit paying on it and find an apartment to rent."

"Thus, the eviction notice on your door." Blu said matter-of-factly.

Her mom nodded, and it seemed a chore for her to gather the courage to continue tallying up what would be needed to get everything current. But she did it, with Blu there trying to be supportive, trying to remind herself that her mom was trying and a lot of this was just the result of the poorer decisions that she'd made in the past—part of what she needed to work through and learn from.

The two women finished with the bills, and Blu had all of the totals and information needed to move forward with a plan for helping her mother. She'd not leave without writing her another check, but she needed to spend a little time thinking about an amount that would be best for her. She didn't want to just swoop in and fix a problem only temporarily, but her mother did seem very determined to check out a few job leads that she'd heard about through some friends of hers; Blu knew that she honestly wasn't looking for a handout. Blu had decided to sleep on it, and they'd sort it out before she left the next day.

They enjoyed the rest of the day together, talking and going for a nice walk in the park across town. Blu took her mom out for a really nice dinner and delighted in how much her mother enjoyed the extravagant meal. She told her about Chase and how much she would love his cooking, already thinking about how nice it would be the next time her mother came to visit them in San Diego. She showed her all of the pictures that she had of Jemma on her phone, both of them laughing at her silly poses and attempts to be funny for the camera.

The day had been very nice, with not a single tear shed or harsh word spoken. For the first time Blu really felt that they'd connected on a different level, and she had no doubts now that their relationship was only going to continue to grow stronger. As she said goodnight, she surprised herself by the touch of sadness that she felt over having to leave the next day. When she'd mentioned it to her mother, Linda had encouraged her to stay longer; but Blu knew that it was time to get back to Jemma, who'd been staying with Claire—and to Chase. She did miss him a lot. They had been talking on the phone every day, but she couldn't wait to catch him up on everything in person.

Blu sat on her mom's worn-out sofa, feet curled underneath her, sipping on the strong coffee she'd made. She was up early—probably due to the slight jet lag she still had—but she didn't mind the time alone before her mom joined her. She had a whirlwind of emotions to process—so much had happened over the past few days. She felt so much peace, it was unbelievable. It was the best she'd felt in a long time by far.

"Good morning." Her mom's cheerful voice interrupted Blu's thoughts.

"Good morning." She grinned. "I hope you don't mind that I helped myself to making some coffee."

"No, not at all. It's lovely to wake up to the smell of fresh coffee. Thank you for that." Her mom laughed, making her way to the kitchen to fill a mug for herself before joining her daughter in the living room.

The two women sat together in easy silence, sipping their coffee. Blu didn't feel the need to speak, and it seemed that her mother felt equally as comfortable with her.

"I really love having you here." Her mother said, breaking the silence. "I'm afraid it's going to seem really weird when you leave, even after such a short time."

Blu nodded, still lost in her own thoughts. She'd woken up that morning with an idea in her head that wouldn't leave her as the morning progressed.

"Blu?"

"Sorry, yes?" Blu said, trying to focus on her mother's words.

"I was just saying that I hope we'll be able to call each other—"

"—Come with me," Blu blurted out without thinking about it a moment longer. "Come with me back to San Diego."

Her mother looked up at her with a surprised expression. "Oh, I couldn't."

"Why not?" Blu said, grinning now. "You can stay with me to begin with—until we sort out if you want your own place or if—if maybe you'd live with us—my place is so big, honestly. There's more than enough room."

Her mother was looking at her with wide eyes. "Really, Blu? Are you being serious with me right now?"

"I am." Blu laughed. "Say yes, just say yes. We'll work everything out as we go. And I can postpone the flight until tomorrow at least."

"I wanna say yes—the idea of it."

"We'll come back to sort out the house and everything later. We'll get your bills caught up so you won't need to worry about that. I know that it's sudden and there are a lot of details to work out, but I really think it could be a good thing," Blu said, her voice rising in excitement.

"I think so too." Her mom was reaching over to pull her into a tight embrace. "A very good thing."

CHAPTER 30

Blu sat next to her mother in first class, enjoying her delight over the roomy seats and special attention. They'd packed up a few things, made a few phone calls, and paid a lot of bills before heading for the airport. And Blu had already purchased another ticket for her mom to be able to come back and finish with her things, shipping whatever she liked to Blu's house in La Jolla. She hadn't mentioned anything yet to her mother, but she was thinking that if she could catch up on some work over the next few days, maybe she and Jemma would join Linda for the trip back.

She looked at her mother, face pressed to the window of the plane as they flew further and further away from New York. Towards a better life for you, Blu thought. She really wanted that for her, and it felt good that she was able to do it for her mother. Out of everything good that had happened to Blu, this was by far the most miraculous.

Her mother turned towards her then, smiling. "Thank

you."

Blu smiled back. "You're welcome. Thank you for agreeing to give my little plan a try."

"Blu, there's nothing little about this." Her mother laughed and then her expression turned serious. "What you're doing—what you've offered me—is life-changing for me."

"I'm happy to do it. It's the right thing to do and it's—it's what I want, too—more than anything now," Blu said.

"I don't just mean the financial bits—and everything amazing that comes with you taking that burden from me—because that is really amazing…"

Blu nodded for her to continue.

"But the opportunity that you're giving me to be back in your life—with you and Jemma—that's something I never imagined could happen. Even when things were good for those few days in San Diego, I never imagined that I'd get to spend much more time with you than that." Her mother was wiping away tears now, obviously choked up, and Blu felt her own tears coming in response.

"You know, this has been a real journey for me too—it's been good for me. Coming out here to see you one more time—that was a total leap of faith for me. Something I never would have done, even six months ago."

Blu's mom reached over to take her hand. "I'm so glad you did."

Blu laughed. "Me too."

Her mother's face was serious again, like there was more she wanted to say.

"What is it?" Blu asked.

"There's something else I want to say to you—I'm not sure that I've expressed it very well at other times lately, and it's important to me."

"Sure." Blu gave her mom's hand a squeeze.

"I had a lot of time to think about you and Jemma while I was in rehab. A lot of things came up for me that I worked out with my therapist there—a lot that I'm still working out. It's hard, you know—dealing with all of the guilt." She looked down for a moment, then took a deep breath, looking like she needed it for the courage to continue.

"I want to thank you, Blu." Her mother looked her in the eyes. "To genuinely thank you for taking Jemma away from me—from Harold." She was crying now, and Blu felt more tears stinging her own eyes as she felt her own wall of guilt coming down, brick by brick, transgression by transgression.

"God knows what would have happened to her." She wiped her hand across her face in a fast, angry motion. "I can't believe that I was so self-consumed, when I was going to prison, that I would have even entertained the idea that Harold could take care of a baby."

"He would not have taken care of her," Blu said, wiping away her own tears at the memory of how she'd found Jemma crying in her crib the day that she'd taken the baby from her mother's house. Harold had been passed out on the sofa, none the wiser that she was even there to relieve him of his duties as father. She'd not even thought about what she was going to do until days after; she swooped up the few clothes, diapers, and other things that she could stuff into her backpack, before swaddling the baby up tight in the one blanket that lay tossed outside the crib. She'd taken her away from there on the bus and never looked back.

"And—" Blu continued in a whisper. "He would have hurt her—once she was old enough." She had known that with every fiber of her being, and she wouldn't have stood by to let Jemma have that kind of start in life. She deserved far better than that.

Her mom was sobbing next to her, and Blu reached to bring her near for a tight hug. "It's okay, Mom. We're both okay."

Her mother looked at her with tear-stained cheeks. "And Jemma—was she okay—when she was a baby, I mean?"

Blu nodded carefully. 'She was fussy, but I didn't have any idea if that was normal or not. I think she was okay, yes."

"I did try so hard once I found out I was pregnant, but it was a few months in before I got help—before I was on the methadone program—I just wondered—I had no idea really if it was too late or—or how that all affected her."

Blu smiled at her, wanting to reassure her now. "Well, I'm not as sure about when she was a baby—I had no real experience with what to expect with that. But I can tell you that she's been what I'd consider a pretty normal kid."

Her mom looked up, her eyes hopeful. "She—she does okay in school then?"

Blu laughed. "Yes, aside from getting in trouble a lot for being too chatty, she makes good grades and does very well when she wants to. Admittedly she's become a bit of a prima donna lately, but that is my doing, not yours." Blu grinned. "I'm hoping maybe that is something you can help me with." Blu winked.

Her mom laughed too. "I'm so relieved to hear all of this. It's haunted me for years, really—that my drug use might have affected her—I'm sure it didn't make things easy on her. I mean, I know that, but I didn't know about the long-term affects—what I might have done to her." Her mom's face lit up then. "But from the little bit of time that I have spent with her, she seems like an absolutely lovely little girl, so I was hopeful—ya know?"

Blu nodded her head, and it was her turn to ask some uncomfortable questions—the details of a few things that they needed to work out before their arrival in San Diego.

"Chase and Jemma are going to meet us at the airport." Blu smiled, happy for the chance for her mother to get to know Chase as well as Jemma. "Jemma was beyond excited when I talked to her last night. Oh, just so you know, she has this idea—of what grandmas do with their grandchildren—that includes a lot of baking. Do you bake cookies?" Blu asked, laughing at her own question.

Her mother laughed too. "No, not really—but I'm certainly willing to give it a try."

Blu continued. "So, I think we should talk about how we are going to handle everything with Jemma—the truth, I mean." Blu looked down at her hands. It was something that she hated to think about. This big lie that she continued to keep from her daughter—from Jemma. *God, do I need to stop thinking of her as my daughter?* The idea seemed foreign to her after all this time. Jemma was her daughter. Blu was the only mother that she'd ever known.

Blu's mother reached out to grab her hand again, squeezing it as she did so. "We can deal with it however you like. I'm not going to do or say anything that doesn't go along with your wishes when it comes to Jemma. I need you to know that."

"I do. I do know that." Blu attempted a smile. "I think—at least for now—we'll just have to let Jemma continue to believe that you are her grandma. God, it's so hard for me to imagine telling her the truth, ya know?" She looked over at her mom.

Her mother nodded her head in agreement. "Well, it would be quite shocking to her—to tell her otherwise—I'm sure."

"Right. But also, as she gets older, it won't be any less shocking." Blu frowned. "I do worry that in the end—if—when I do tell her—she's going to hate me."

"No, Blu. She won't hate you. We'll make sure of that—that she knows the whole truth. I'll always be okay with that." She was nodding her head strongly as she spoke, the determination written on her face. "We don't have to sugarcoat anything in terms of the part I played in all of this. I will never have you be taken for the bad guy in any of this. Ever."

Blu nodded. "I hope you're right. About her not hating me, I mean."

"We'll just do the best we can. That's all we can do, right?" her mother said.

Blu nodded and the two women spent the remainder of the flight in silence, Blu thinking about her sins of omission, and her mother—Blu guessed—lost in her own thoughts about the past and this new future they were trying to figure out together.

CHAPTER 31

Blu snuck up behind Chase in the kitchen, putting her arms around his waist while peering around him at the sauce bubbling on the stove. "That smells delicious."

He gave the sauce one more stir before turning around to kiss her neck, breathing in deeply through his nose. "You smell delicious, my darling."

She laughed as his light kisses tickled her neck before he planted one long deep kiss on her lips.

"Do you think we have time to sneak upstairs quick?" Chase winked at her and she laughed, delighted with his teasing.

"You be good." She grinned.

He put a lid on the pot, turning the heat down low for it to simmer, then took Blu by the hand, leading her over to the window. He wrapped his arms around her small frame, pulling her in close, kissing her cheek as they both looked out at their friends gathered on the deck.

Gigi and Douglas stood off to the side, each with one arm around the other, each with their free hand holding a glass of wine as they toasted to something that looked particularly serious and lovely. Their smiles were wide, a look of hope and infinite possibilities as they looked out towards the ocean, lost in conversation—the picture of being in love.

Lia, Antonio, and Victoria looked engrossed in a conversation that Blu suspected had to do with her friend's upcoming anniversary trip to Italy. She'd been talking with her husband about wanting to get to Tuscany, and finally he'd agreed to take the time off work to celebrate their tenth anniversary, an occasion Victoria felt very much deserved such a trip.

Blu's attention turned to Jemma, Claire, and her mother Linda, seated at another table, the three of them giggling hysterically at something that Blu imagined the two girls had done to win her mom's laughter and delight—something that Blu had seen daily since the moment her mom had arrived to stay with them nearly two months ago.

Blu turned her face towards Chase's for another kiss, a sigh of pure contentment escaping her mouth as she thought of everything that had happened over the past few months. "I really can't believe how happy I am," she said.

"I love how happy you are," Chase said and laughed lightly. "You're beautiful all the time, but especially when you're happy," he teased.

Blu laughed. "I'm just still pinching myself at how great everything has worked out, ya know? With my mother, I mean—and with you, of course—but that's a given."

He squeezed her tighter to him. "It is pretty remarkable. Your mother is really lovely. And I've seen her with Jemma—while they've been working. It's something she's really great at, I'd say."

"You think so too? I didn't have anything to compare it too, but I've thought the same thing myself—a hidden talent of my mother's, I'd say."

Blu had made a lot of decisions over the past few months—as had her mother—coming to the conclusion that they wanted to try homeschooling Jemma together, in preparation for the travel—and some big changes—that would be in Blu's near future. She really did want to take Jemma with her, and now she wanted her mother there also—to be able to share these experiences with her—with both of them. And Chase would join them whenever he could. He'd assured her of that, and had been doing his best to open up his schedule just a bit more.

The two looked at one another, instantaneously agreeing that it was time to hand out the champagne. The evening was perfect, the sunset magnificent. Blu and Chase made their way to their guests, Blu delivering the sparkling cider to the girls, her mother, and herself, while Chase handed out the glasses of the fine bottle of champagne he'd splurged on for the occasion.

Blu looked around, tears in her eyes, before speaking to the people around her—her family. And tonight she was especially grateful as she looked towards her mother with her arms around Jemma.

"Thank you all for coming. It's always such a pleasure to have you here and tonight I'm—" Chase came up beside her, taking her hand in his. "—we're very grateful to have you here with us—for you all to meet Linda—my mother." Blu raised her glass towards her mom, all at once too choked up, as she saw her mom wiping her own tears away, to finish her toast.

Blu nodded at Douglas, who seemed eager to say something.

"Well, I would also like to say a thank you to Blu and Chase, always the most lovely of hosts, and give our warmest welcome to Linda—and my wife and I have a little announcement that we'd like to share with you all."

Gigi was grinning like the cat who had swallowed the canary as Douglas put his arm around her, squeezing her to him. Everyone else waited in expectation for Douglas to continue, including Blu—who had an inkling as Gigi sent a discreet wink her way.

"I've finally set a retirement date for later this year so that I can give this wonderful woman here the life she deserves—if that happens to include spending more time with this ol geezer." He laughed at his own joke as Gigi playfully swatted his arm and then grabbed him for a kiss as the rest of the gang erupted into claps and shouts of "congratulations".

Blu saw a look pass between Antonio and Lia, who

were standing right next to her. She whispered into her friend's ear. "Go on if you have an announcement to make too," she teased, knowing full well by the look on her friend's face that they did.

After the cheers had lessened, Lia cleared her throat and took Antonio by the hand. "Douglas, Antonio and I are so happy for you both, and we hope that some of those retirement plans have to do with long visits to Italy." Lia smiled as Gigi nodded an emphatic yes.

Lia continued. "At the risk of trying to one-up you two in the announcement department—but I mean, come on, how often are we all together like this to be able to celebrate?" Everyone laughed, especially Blu, who couldn't agree more. Lia and Antonio looked at each other, smiling, a silent agreement passing between them that it was Antonio's turn to speak now.

"I've asked Lia to be my wife and she said yes." Antonio brought Lia's hand to his lips for a gentle kiss.

"And of course you will all be invited to our wedding at the vineyard."

More cheers and hugs all around as the words of congratulations flowed freely. Blu thought that Lia looked the happiest that she'd ever seen her.

And Blu realized something as she looked around at these people, at her mother laughing with Jemma—her mother, who had become such a big part of her life—of Jemma's life. She realized that maybe this was the happiest that she'd ever been. The one person missing was Arianna; but especially tonight, amidst all of the great announcements, Arianna's presence was a thing that Blu felt—that she was sure they all felt.

As she basked in the happy announcements of her friends, Blu felt Chase's arms come around her to rest on the slight bump of her small belly. She turned around to kiss him on the lips and whispered in his ear. "It's okay. We'll make our announcement later." She grinned up at him as he nodded in agreement, pulling her close, loving her like she'd never been loved before.

ABOUT THE AUTHOR

Paula Kay spent her childhood in a small town alongside the Mississippi River in Wisconsin. (Go Packers!) As a child, she used to climb the bluffs and stare out across the mighty river—dreaming of far away lands and adventures.

Today, by some great miracle (and a lot of determination) she is able to travel, write and live in multiple locations, always grateful for the opportunity to meet new people and experience new cultures.

She enjoys Christian music, long chats with friends, reading (and writing) books that make her cry and just a tad too much reality TV.

Paula loves to hear from her readers and can be contacted via her website where you can also download a complimentary book of short stories.

PaulaKayBooks.com

ALL TITLES BY PAULA KAY

http://Amazon.com/author/paulakay

The Complete Legacy Series

Buying Time
In Her Own Time
Matter of Time
Taking Time
Just in Time
All in Good Time

Visit the author website at PaulaKayBooks.com to get on the notification list for new releases and special offers—and to also receive the complimentary download of "The Bridge: A Collection of Short Stories."

Made in the USA
Monee, IL
07 November 2022

17330757R00138